D0403742

DRAGON WARS

· THUNDER IN GUNDER ·

— BOOK 5 —

CRAIG HALLORAN

DON'T FORGET YOUR FREE BOOKS

Join my newsletter and receive three magnificent stories from my bestselling series for FREE!

Not to mention that you'll have direct access to my collection of over 80 books, including audiobooks and boxsets. FREE and .99 cents eBook giveaways galore!

Sign up here!
WWW.DRAGONWARSBOOKS.COM

Finally, please leave a review of Thunder in Gunder - Book 5 when you finish. I've typed my fingers to the bone writing it and your reviews are a huge help!
THUNDER IN GUNDER REVIEW LINK

Dragon Wars: Thunder in Gunder - Book 5

By Craig Halloran

★★★★

Copyright © 2019 by Craig Halloran

Amazon Edition

TWO-TEN BOOK PRESS

PO Box 4215, Charleston, WV 25364

ISBN eBook: 978-1-946218-74-2

ISBN Paperback: 978-1-654682-78-1

ISBN Hardback: 978-1-946218-75-9

www.craighalloran.com

All rights reserved. No part of this publication may be reproduced, stored in a retrieval system, or transmitted in any form or by any means—electronic, mechanical, recorded, photocopied, or otherwise—without the prior permission of the copyright owner, except by a reviewer who may quote brief passages in a review.

Publisher's Note

This book is a work of fiction. Names, characters, places, and incidents either are the product of the author's imagination or are used fictitiously, and any resemblance to actual persons, living or dead, events, or locales is entirely coincidental.

 Created with Vellum

1

DAGGERFORD

Bowbreaker's steed raced across the moonlit countryside north of Daggerford. The strapping elven ranger bent over the horse's neck, his jet-black hair streaming behind him like a banner. He spoke into the animal's ear, using special words that only the rangers of his craft knew. "Goitah! Goitah!"

The lathered horse snorted. Its stride lengthened, and its hooves thundered over the packed ground.

"Goitah! Goitah! Goitah!" Bowbreaker repeated. He chanced a look over his shoulder.

Cutting through the night, only a few horse lengths behind him, was the Doom Rider named Ghost. The menacing foe wore a leather skull mask and dragon-scale-leather armor and rode a supernatural dragon-horse called a gourn. The gourn's eyes shined bright with fire, and hot smoke streamed from its nostrils. They were closing in.

Minutes earlier, Bowbreaker had split from the company called Talon. He had hoped to lead the Doom Riders and the Scourge away from their pursuit or to divide their forces. Only Ghost had fallen for the ploy. Bowbreaker had tangled with the Doom Rider back in Daggerford. The frightening pursuer had shrugged off mortal wounds like a dog shed water.

Bowbreaker turned his mount from the beaten path into the woodland. The horse jumped the thickets and powered through the brush. They zigzagged through the trees, branches and leaves whipping their faces.

"Goitah! Goitah!" Bowbreaker had full command of his horse. Being a ranger, he was a master of many animals and could push them beyond their means. Such was the case now, as the gourn, a powerful monster, pursued them with the skill and grace of a stag.

The horse jumped a log, landed hard, and jostled Bowbreaker so hard that his foot came out of the stirrup. He fought to regain control and jammed his foot back in place. They splashed through a stream, a seam of moonlight twinkling on its surface offering a moment of light before they plunged back into the forest.

Bowbreaker considered his options as he felt his horse laboring beneath him. They'd been sprinting for over a league. His horse couldn't handle much more. Bowbreaker had a quiver on his back but no bow. His sword bounced beside his saddle, and a hunting knife was tucked into his belt. He would be no match for the Doom Rider and a gourn. In order to survive, it would take something special.

"Goitah! Goitah!"

Closing his eyes, he puckered his lips and whistled. The sound was nearly drowned out by the pounding of horse hooves and rustling of branches. The whistle grew louder, weaving into the calm night like a sea siren's call that would prick the ears of sailors.

The deeper they plunged into the forest, the more the forest came to life as critters jumped and raced across the branches. From out of their burrows and knotholes, they came: birds, chipmunks, black squirrels.

Bowbreaker opened his eyes and slowed to a trot. So did his pursuer.

The varmints raced over the branches. Swarms of birds darted from the treetops. Dozens of squirrels and chipmunks jumped from the ends of the branches and covered Ghost like a pelt. Night birds and woodpeckers landed on the gourn's head and pecked at its eyes. The frightening beast reared up, and flames shot out of its mouth as it shook its great neck. The critters and birds piled onto the enemies, covering them in a blanket of fur and feathers.

Bowbreaker continued with his eerie ranger whistle and urged his horse back into a full gallop. The woodland creatures bought him the time he needed. He stretched the distance between himself and the angry growls of the gourn. Several thunderous horse steps later, his horse burst out of the woodland and onto the plains. He turned the beast and rode along the woodland's edge.

Every branch and tree he passed rattled with life as the critters came to his aid.

Behind him, Ghost and the gourn burst from the woods, both wearing biting critters for coats. More critters crowded the gourn's path, and birds dove at their heads from the sky. The juggernaut barely slowed. Fur and bird feathers went everywhere.

Bowbreaker's horse couldn't go on much longer. The beast's breaths began to rattle in its throat. He wouldn't let his horse die on his account. He slowed the beast, grabbed his sword, and jumped off.

The horse kept running.

He dashed into the woodland, still whistling, searched for a place to hide in the great trees, and climbed. His spell, the ranger's whistle, lost its potency and died. The varmints retreated to their burrows, and the birds flew back to their nests.

Ghost plowed into the forest and brought his gourn to a walk as the forest quieted.

If Bowbreaker had brought his bow, he could have shot the Doom Rider in the skull. He had the perfect shot from his perch in the branches, twenty feet above.

Ghost slowed to a stop. His head turned from shoulder

to shoulder. He eyed the ground and slid off his gourn. The gourn cast a glow over the ground as its great nostrils flared and sniffed. Using a front paw, it clawed at the dirt.

Bowbreaker's temple pounded. He'd faced many foes but never the likes of the Doom Rider and a gourn. They were renowned for their strength, power, and skill. Alone, or even with his weapon of choice, the long bow, he was no match for them. His only hope was to hide and survive, but if it failed, he took solace in that his efforts may have saved his friends. That was all that mattered.

Ghost took the gourn by the reins and led it into the dark greenery of the woodland.

Bowbreaker could barely hear their soft footfalls pass over the forest floor. He watched until the glow of the gourn's eyes vanished into the trees. He waited several more minutes then climbed down. Pausing at the base of the tree, he checked all directions, but before he took a step, a sword blade whistled through the air and chopped at his throat. His life flashed before his eyes. It was over.

2

Ranger instinct saved Bowbreaker as he sank to his knees in the wink of an eye. The sword chopped into the tree over his head.

Ghost, once invisible, reappeared right before Bowbreaker's eyes. The Doom Rider fought to wrench free the sword that would have decapitated Bowbreaker a moment before.

From a crouch, Bowbreaker kicked Ghost's legs out from under him. The pair wrestled through the woodland. Bowbreaker fought with sword and knife, trying to bring his sword down on Ghost's head. With his hunting knife in his right hand, Bowbreaker gouged a deep gash in Ghost's thigh.

The rangy fighter didn't utter a word or gasp in pain. Instead, he locked his fingers on Bowbreaker's wrist and twisted the dagger back toward its owner. Ghost rolled on top of Bowbreaker and knocked the sword free from his grip. Using both hands, Ghost twisted the knife over Bowbreaker's chest and pushed down.

Bowbreaker's right arm, the arm that plucked the bowstring, was stronger than iron. The muscles bulged and flexed underneath his tanned skin. Even with Ghost using two arms, his own arm didn't budge. With his left hand, he repeatedly punched Ghost in the jaw.

Whap! Whap! Whap!

The chin of Ghost's skull mask went askew.

He felt Ghost's cold, fetid breath on his face. There was something about Ghost's nature that made his skin crawl. The man was a living sickness in a human body, strong as iron yet sick as a dog. With his jaw clenched, Bowbreaker stared into the Doom Rider's brown, almost-black eyes. He saw his struggling expression in them. He punched again.

Whap! Whap! Whap!

Bowbreaker's knuckles felt like they were hitting stone.

The knife dipped closer to his chest. He thrust back.

Ghost, the silent killer, put his full weight behind the knife. The blade dipped into Bowbreaker's buckskin shirt.

With his free hand, Bowbreaker grabbed Ghost's mask and pulled it off. His eyes widened.

Ghost was an orc, which explained the strapping build. But he was different. His skin was pale, almost translucent, and blue veins streaked his face. The once-coarse head of black hair had thinned and faded. Much like a swamp walker, he appeared to live between life and death, with little to no apparent humanity. It explained why mortal weapons did him little harm.

Bowbreaker shoved back hard against the blade once more. Ghost's arms didn't budge. His strength was more than orcen. It was supernatural. With the palm of his hand, Bowbreaker shoved Ghost's chin backward.

The gourn returned. It looked down at Bowbreaker and huffed hot, steamy breath on his face. The breath became hotter and hotter.

Sweat beaded on Bowbreaker's burning face. He let out a scream.

Ghost pushed down, piercing Bowbreaker's shoulder with his own hunting knife. He cried out again. He was beaten. He only hoped his sacrifice was worth it. To his surprise, Ghost removed the knife, put on his mask, and hauled Bowbreaker to his feet. Bowbreaker winced as the Doom Rider bound his hands behind his back. Ghost shoved him forward and started marching him out of the forest.

Bowbreaker would rather die than be taken prisoner.

A scuffle deep in the woodland caught his ear. The fight wasn't over yet. Something huge lumbered though the thatches and thistles toward them. From between the towering maple trees, a massive bear emerged. The gray hackles on its back raised up like razors. Its eyes locked on the gourn, and it let out the wild cry of the king of the forest.

Ghost and the gourn turned to face the bear.

The bear rose on its hind legs and stretched to its towering ten-foot height. It looked down on them all, its heavy eyes filled with intense anger.

Bowbreaker almost managed a smile. The silver-backed grizzly was better than what he'd hoped for when he used the ranger's whistle. The timing couldn't have been better. He looked back at Ghost and said, "Say hello to my furry little friend."

The grizzly and the gourn charged. The grizzly plowed past the gourn's flaming mouth and tackled the monster to the ground. They crashed through small trees, snapping them in half as their massive bodies thrashed over the woodland.

Bowbreaker caught Ghost watching the fight. He launched a hard backward kick straight into the orc's belly, doubling the orc over. Bowbreaker started running. With the gourn distracted, the fleet-footed ranger saw his best chance to get away on foot.

Ghost proved fast, but an orc in a footrace against an elf would never be a match, even with the elf's arms tied behind his back.

Small branches whipped across his face as Bowbreaker's legs churned, carrying him toward the sound of water. He made it to a shallow creek and turned downstream. He made it half a league down the waterway before he heard the roar of a gourn. He took a quick over-the-shoulder look.

Ghost was back on top of the gourn, riding hard in Bowbreaker's direction.

Apparently, the silver-back grizzly couldn't hold off the gourn long enough, or he died trying. Bowbreaker hoped not. He raced on, pushing himself to his limits, listening for the sound of a waterfall crashing ahead. He knew the territory and understood where the waters ran. The edge of the forest was coming, and a steep cliff was waiting.

Ghost bore down on him and closed the gap quickly.

Bowbreaker felt the dragon-horse's hot breath on his back. The end of the stream was near. The water's edge vanished over a black gap and crashed downward, far, far below. With the wind in his face and a gourn on his back, he took his last ten strides and jumped into the blackness, where cold water and jagged rocks waited to swallow him down below.

3

MONARCH CITY

"Are we almost there?" Grey Cloak asked Crane. He was lying in the flatbed of the wagon, which bumped and rocked from side to side. The wagon suddenly jumped, and his head banged on the board below. "Ow! Are you trying to ride over every rut?"

From the front bench, Crane twisted his shoulders over his big belly to look at Grey Cloak. "Almost there. Be patient." He had short, kinky brown hair and a warm expression like a puppy dog. "Enjoy the ride."

"Yes, enjoy the ride. All you've been doing is complaining," Zora said. The young half-elf woman sat beside Crane with a playful smile on her full lips. She was petting the runt dragon, Streak, who lay on her lap. "Even Streak has tired of your griping."

"I'm not complaining," Grey Cloak said as he looked up

at the cloudy sky, which up until recently, had been clear and sunny. "I wish all of you would quit saying that."

"You did it again," Dyphestive said. He lay in the wagon, too, with his head at the opposite end from Grey Cloak's. His big head was resting in his strong, calloused hands.

"Did what again?" Grey Cloak asked.

"Complained," Dyphestive replied.

Grey Cloak sat up straight. "Are you saying that me saying that I wish all of you would stop telling me to stop complaining is a complaint?"

All at the same time, Dyphestive, Zora, and Crane said, "Yes." Even Streak managed a little squawk.

"Ridiculous. Will someone help me out here?" He looked to Tanlin for help. The older scarf-wearing rogue rode horseback. He shrugged his eyebrows at Grey Cloak. Cotton, the venerable halfling riding with Tanlin, didn't say a word. "Thanks for nothing."

"You like to bellyache for the sake of bellyaching." Rhonna, the dwarven blacksmith, was sharing a saddle with Lythlenion and riding behind the orcen cleric. "You always did."

Grey Cloak touched his chest and gave her a look of shock. "I can't imagine why I would ever complain around you. I mean, after all of the backbreaking, character-testing chores, why would I ever complain about anything?" Ramping up the sarcasm, he said, "If I could only go back to Havenstock, where you work my elven fingers to the bone, mending fences, rustling cattle, shoveling out stables." He kicked Dyphestive's shoulder with is toe. "My brother and I enjoyed those menial tasks so very, very much. Pulling the plows, shucking the corn, milking the cows, hours before dawn. And yet you complain that I complain."

"Complaining can be healthy," Lythlenion said cheerfully. "It relieves your anxious behavior."

"Thank you." Grey Cloak gave a sweeping bow. "Finally, someone understands my anxiousness to arrive at our point of destination."

"I'm glad we're back together, brother. I missed your complaining," Dyphestive said.

Zora chuckled.

"Stitch it up, pumpkin head." Grey Cloak slapped Dyphestive on the knee and smiled. "I missed you too. How are you feeling?"

"I'm glad but feel very guilty." Dyphestive stole a glance at Cotton. "I'm empty. I can't ever right a wrong like that. I swear, I don't think I should ever pick up a weapon again. I can't bear the thought of hurting another person."

Grey Cloak pulled his knees up to his chest and nodded. "When we get to Monarch City, we'll stay out of trouble."

"I don't see how. We're wanted men," Dyphestive replied.

"We'll lie low and blend in. It's easy to get lost in a massive place like Monarch City, isn't it, Crane?"

"So long as you don't upset the wrong people, you should be fine," Crane replied. "But if you do, they'll send the Honor Guard after you."

The horse-drawn wagon, pulled by the horse Vixen rolled up over a rise and down the other side. Zora gasped. Dyphestive sat up, and Grey Cloak turned toward the front as Crane brought the wagon to a halt.

"Whoa, Vixen, whoa," Crane said.

Grey Cloak stood up in the wagon. Dyphestive joined him.

"What is that?" Grey Cloak asked.

"A dragonlith," Crane said, his gaze attached to the foreign structure. "Isn't she beautiful?"

The wagon rocked and groaned as Dyphestive hopped out. "It's humongous."

Grey Cloak picked up Streak and climbed out of the wagon. His eyes never left the dragonlith that stared back at them like a hawk. "I don't know that 'humongous' is adequate."

Perched on a column of black stone that must have been one hundred feet wide and fifty feet tall was the perfect image of a dragon sitting with its wings spread half-open and its tail coiled around its feet. The dragon itself stood another fifty feet high and appeared bigger than the great column it was perched upon. Every detail of the dragon was finely carved, from scale to claw. The dragon was covered in a veneer that made every detail, from the eyes and horns to the scales, look astonishingly real.

Grey Cloak caught his breath. He'd never seen an image of a dragon so big. It dwarfed the likes of Cinder by comparison. As if compelled by their own free will, his feet made their way down the hill toward the dragonlith.

Streak's throat rattled.

"I know, he is very big." Grey Cloak stared up into the dragon's eyes, which appeared to stare back down into his.

Dyphestive caught up with him. The others filed in from behind.

The dragonlith was surrounded by lush flowerbeds, woodland, and greenery as far as the eye could see. Huge dogwood trees with rose petals circled the dragonlith's base but were dwarfed by comparison. Paths and trails led to the dragonlith from all directions. The area was quiet and peaceful, and not a single bird alighted on the dragon.

"What is it doing here?" Grey Cloak's eyes broke away from the monument and scanned their surroundings.

"It's been here for as long as anyone can remember, built by worshippers back in the day when dragons ruled all of Gapoli," Crane said, with bright eyes. "Look at her. She's as perfect as the day she was created. So majestic. So real."

"Yes, the gilding and veneer are quite impressive,"

Tanlin said as he untied the knot in his scarf. "They say the dragonliths were created to protect us."

"Protect us from what?" Zora asked.

Tanlin shrugged. "Any threat that befalls us. Of course, it's just a legend."

For some reason, Grey Cloak found Tanlin's words haunting, and his stomach fluttered. He thought about Anya and wondered how she and Cinder were getting along. *I hope Cinder isn't still sleeping in a snowbank.*

"Well, you've all seen the dragonlith. I thought it would be worth showing to you on our way to Monarch City"—Crane glanced at Grey Cloak—"which is only a few leagues away?"

Grey Cloak climbed back in the wagon. "What are we waiting for? Once we get there, I'll purchase a feast for us all."

"Not all of us," Rhonna stated as she huffed on a cigar. The look on her face was as serious as ever. "I'm going back to Havenstock."

4

"R honna, you can't leave now," Grey Cloak said, jumping back out of the wagon.

Dyphestive grabbed the reins to Lythlenion's horse. "She's not going anywhere."

"Don't be foolish," Rhonna said. She took a swipe at Dyphestive from where she sat in the saddle behind Lythlenion. "Let go."

"No," Dyphestive said like a pouting child.

Rhonna let out an audible sigh. "Horseshoes. One would think that you'd be glad to get rid of me."

"Why are you leaving?" Grey Cloak asked as the others assembled around the dwarf. "Why now?"

Rhonna climbed out of the saddle, sucked on the cigar, and released a stream of white smoke. "I left Havenstock to find the both of you," she said to Grey Cloak and Dyphestive. "I succeeded, somehow. Now both of you are safe and free, and you don't need me anymore. You're men now, a bit young but no longer striplings. You can handle life on your own."

Grey Cloak took a knee, and Dyphestive joined him. "But we are a team. We are Talon, and you're our leader."

"No, I'm not the leader of this band, I'm afraid. I might have been for a spell, but well, I'm too old for this," she said.

"Well, you're old, yes, but not that old," Grey Cloak said.

Zora took a knee in the grass. "Rhonna, please stay. We need you."

"It's my time," Rhonna said, "and Lyth's too."

"Lyth! You're going too?" Dyphestive asked.

With a sad look, Lythlenion said, "I adore all of you, but I miss my wife and daughter horribly. It's time for me."

Grey Cloak's jaw hung open as Streak climbed back into his hood. Grey Cloak shook his head in disbelief. "I really can't believe you're going. I'd rather you stayed, Rhonna, even though you are a hardhead."

"You're more than welcome to come back to the forge," she said.

He lifted his hands. "No, no, I'll take my chances in Monarch City. If it doesn't work out, I may return for a visit."

"Of course we'll return for a visit." Dyphestive nodded. "All of us. I wouldn't mind plowing a few fields again. It's nothing compared to what the Doom Riders put me through."

"Or what the Sky Riders put me through." Grey Cloak's gaze met Rhonna's. "Our time in Havenstock served us well, Rhonna. I'm grateful you took us in," he admitted.

"Me too," Dyphestive said.

Rhonna's eyes started to water, and she said, "Don't get soggy on me now."

Dyphestive wrapped her up in a bear hug. "I love you, Rhonna!"

"Horseshoes, will you stop blubbering? You're too big for that," she replied as she hugged him back.

Zora started to cry. "Oh, my heart is breaking."

"I know the timing is awful," Tanlin said as he put the Scarf of Shadows over Zora's shoulders.

Zora jumped to her feet. "Tanlin, what are you doing?" She tried to force the scarf back into his hands.

Tanlin locked his hands over hers. "I'm going back to Raven Cliff. I'm not fit for these adventures anymore. I can feel it in my bones. I don't have it in me."

"Of course you do," Zora said. "You are the best. You taught me all that I know."

"You flatter me, but it's time. I was all but worthless back in Daggerford when dealing with the Doom Riders."

"That's not true. You've always told me that even the smallest part can have the greatest impact."

"I know. I'm not departing because I feel I'm a failure.

I'm leaving because I know that it's time for me to serve in another manner more suitable to my wizened strength." Tanlin tied the scarf around Zora's neck. "I want you to have this."

"No, I don't—"

"Zora, you are the daughter I never had. It's a gift. I want you to keep it. Besides, you know where our home is."

She buried her head in his shoulder and cried.

Lythlenion nudged Dyphestive with his war mace. "I want you to have this, young fella. It's very suitable to your build."

"No, I couldn't," Dyphestive said.

Lythlenion dropped the war mace on the ground. "I'm leaving Thunderash. It's up to you whether you take it or not. But I want you to have it. Please."

Dyphestive swallowed the lump in his throat and nodded. "Well, who else is leaving? What about you, Cotton?"

"I think I'll stay with Tanlin, if he'll have me," Cotton said quietly.

"Of course," Tanlin replied.

"You aren't going to leave us at Monarch City's doorstep. Are you, Crane?" Grey Cloak asked.

"Heavens, no. I'm going to Monarch City, where the women are all kinds of pretty," Crane said, with his usual whimsical smile. "Now, pile in. I'm starting to get hungry."

The members of Talon went their separate ways without a dry eye among them.

Grey Cloak waved goodbye to Rhonna. "If any more orphan runaways show up, go easy on them, will you?"

Rhonna shouted back. "Never!"

5

Grey Cloak and company faced the West Link, the bridge joining Westerlund to Monarch City. He drank from a canteen to wet his dry throat and handed the canteen back to Dyphestive. Standing behind Crane and Zora, who rode in the front of the wagon, he placed a hand on each of their shoulders. "That's a bridge? How can a bridge be so big? I can barely see to the other side."

"That's only the West Link. There are three more, the North, the South, and the East Link." Crane flicked his carriage whip. Vixen pulled the wagon toward the bridge entrance, which was surrounded by soldiers inspecting everyone coming from and going to the city. "Those soldiers are in the Honor Guard—the finest troops in the land, represented by every race and territory. They are a melting pot of Gapoli's finest, making them the very best, so behave yourselves."

The Honor Guard wore scale armor with matching thigh and shin guards that glinted in the sun. Ornamental metal skullcaps covered their heads and swept down past their necks. The men were clean-shaven, and the women tied back their hair in tight braids or wore it short. Their rank and status could be noted by the golden-yellow sash that they wore. Each man and woman was well armed with a sword or spear, and all of them carried small steel bucklers.

A male soldier from the Honor Guard stopped the wagon.

Crane gave the customary greetings while a female soldier walked around the wagon. She was part elf, and her hard stare scanned everything in, on, or around the wagon. Her eyes lingered on Dyphestive longer than most before she moved on.

Grey Cloak scooted closer to his brother. "Did you see her hungry look? I think she fancies you."

Dyphestive blushed. "Don't be silly. She wasn't." He twisted his head around to look at the soldier. "Was she?"

"Why didn't I see it before? Of course, that's not the reason. It must be because you are so big that you take twice as long to look at," Grey Cloak joked.

"Ha ha," Dyphestive replied. He checked out his arms

and body and lifted his blond eyebrows. "But I suppose that could be true."

"Welcome to Monarch City. Behave yourselves," the male soldier said. "Stay right."

With a snap of the wrist, Crane led the company toward the bridge.

Grey Cloak eyeballed the battle towers that guarded the wide bridge's entrance. Each stone tower was a hundred feet high and fortified with archers, crossbowmen, and soldiers manning ballistae. At the base of each tower were garrisons of soldiers performing their daily duties.

The wagon bumped over the gap where the bridge joined with the land. The bridge road was at least fifty yards wide and made of rows and rows of timber planks. The wheels rattled over the wood.

"If you look over the wall, you can see the moat. Fresh water and full of the biggest freshwater fish you ever saw." Crane stood up and looked over the edge. "I even saw a mermaid down there once. We were going to get married. She proposed to me."

Crane started spitting out random trivia. "If an army charged across these bridges, the bottom would fall out on them. Monarch City can sustain itself for decades. It's impossible to siege. The wine tastes like honey, and the honey tastes like wine. If you stare at a Monarch too long, you'll be cast into the dungeons. The chickens are so big that they hunt the foxes. Beware of the Dark Addler.

Always check your pockets. Don't eat at Joseph's. Watch out for the waterfall. Beggars *can* be choosers when you know your way around here. The moat is deep, but the lies are deeper."

Grey Cloak hopped out of the wagon and walked closer to the bridge's edge. The walkway near the wall was made of red stone, and the decorative wall was made of white sandstone. He looked over the wall, which stood no higher than his chest, toward the blue waters below. The moat was surrounded by cliff faces over two hundred feet high. Inside the moat were ships like the ones that could be seen on a fishing lake. Their sails were colored, full of wind, and they moved quickly over the waters.

He dusted the hair from his eyes. He couldn't figure out where the breeze came from that filled the sails of the fishing boats below, but it was brisk and steady. The air was fresh, and the scent of flowers intermingled with the breeze. He closed his eyes, took a deep breath, and let out a sigh.

A warm presence approached his side.

He smiled. "Hello, Zora."

6

"Well now, it seems that my days of sneaking up on you are over," Zora said.

"It would seem so." Grey Cloak casually leaned on the wall. "Either that or you are slipping."

"That would make better sense, but I'm not slipping. I can assure you of that," she quipped.

"Your heavy breathing sold you out."

"I wasn't breathing heavy."

He smirked. "Come now, Zora. It's been a long time since you've seen me. It's perfectly understandable."

She pinched his arm and twisted.

"Ow!" He rubbed his arm. "Why did you do that?"

"Because I wanted to try and pop your bloated head."

"My head's not bloated... that much."

"No, it isn't. Only a little fat between the temples," she said.

"I missed you, too, Zora," he said.

She held his hand and pulled him after the wagon. "Come on, we better catch up before Crane loses us. And yes, I missed you. Very much."

He fought the urge to say "I know," as he wanted to keep ahold of her warm hand. Perhaps he had matured and learned to bridle his tongue better. He decided to take another approach. "That's a nice scarf that Tanlin gave you."

"He should have kept it, not me. I don't deserve it."

"Of course you do."

She petted the dark scarf with her free hand. "You know, I've always fancied it. I never said it, but perhaps he knew."

"You're a thief. I don't think that desire would surprise him."

"No, I don't suppose it would, but I would do the same for him."

He nodded. "Would you do the same for me? I really like it."

"Ha ha. No, not unless I was dying. Then, maybe." She tightened her grip on his hand and leaned on his shoulder.

Warmth flooded through him, and his heart began to race. *Zooks. Perhaps I really have changed.*

"I really miss him," she said as they slowly caught up to

the wagon, where Dyphestive had climbed into the front seat. He looked like an ogre sitting beside Crane. "I'm worried."

"I know. I'm sure I'll miss Tanlin too." He squeezed her hand. "But I wouldn't worry. Rhonna and Lythlenion will get him safely back to Raven Cliff."

Zora shook her head gently. "I'm not worried about Tanlin. I'm worried about Bowbreaker."

"Bowbreaker?"

"Yes, I'm sad that I'll never see him again, and he could be hurt."

What?

"Uh, I'm sure that he's fine. Very capable with his bow, fingers and all."

"Do you think he's handsome?"

"Huh?" He scratched his head with his free hand. "I suppose, if you like elves who wash in the woodland and frolic with animals."

Zora stopped, broke her grip, and glared into his eyes. "What is that supposed to mean?"

"It means that he's not civilized like you and me. He's a woodsman, a ranger. They are a different breed." He shook his head. "I don't think that you and he would be well suited. He doesn't even talk."

"Well, some men talk too much." She poked his chest. "And who are you to judge him. He's brave, strong, and has a muscular chest."

Grey Cloak flexed his arms. "I'm brave and strong. And"—he lifted his finger—"I have a dragon."

"You don't understand. I really like him. We"—her stare drifted to the sky—"connected."

"Oh." His shoulders sunk. "I see."

"Grey Cloak," she said as she hooked his arm with both of hers, "I'm sorry. I didn't mean to give you the wrong impression. I need your comfort as a friend. And you are very young, a man but still very young."

"You can't be that much older. I realize that our crow's feet are premature..."

"Crow's feet!" She crushed his arm in hers. "You take that back."

"Then I'd be lying."

"You're lying now, you elven hound."

Even though he felt his heart collapsing, he played along with her and bayed like a hound.

She tried to cover his mouth. "Will you stop that? People are looking."

Even though he hurt inside, he howled again. Zora tried to silence him using both hands.

He scooped her up in his strong arms and tossed her into the wagon like a child.

"Oh," she said with wide eyes as she rubbed her rump. "You're stronger than I figured."

He sprang into the wagon like a gazelle and set his eyes ahead. "I know."

The wagon rolled by columns and garrisons similar to the ones on the opposite end of the bridge. More of the Honor Guard greeted them and scanned the wagon before waving them on.

They faced miles of countryside with farm-rich fields and roaming livestock as far as the eye could see. Stone cottages were scattered all across the rolling hills.

"Crops aplenty, everyone! Crops aplenty!" Crane said.

"Where's Monarch City?" Dyphestive asked with a puzzled look. "This looks like another territory."

"That's the beauty of it. Monarch City is its own territory, the same as Westerlund, Arrowwood, or Valley Shire. The only difference is that it's surrounded by a huge moat, so to speak," Crane offered. "Don't fret. You'll see the shining spires before you know it, and trust me when I say you'll never forget them. There is nothing quite like your first adventure to Monarch City." He leaned into Dyphestive. "Figuratively speaking." He pointed to a nearby heard grazing in the fields. "Look at those cows. I'm mad about cows. I love them."

Grey Cloak, Dyphestive, and Zora exchanged funny looks but kept their laughter to themselves.

The sun had started to set, and the wagon wheels rolled over the sweeping countryside that didn't appear to end. In the distance, a bright glint of sunlight caught Grey Cloak's eye. He stood up in the wagon and pulled Zora up by the hand. Their mouths hung open.

Monarch City waited on the horizon, a dazzling marvel made of white stone buildings and cobalt-blue and brick-red rooftops. The buildings dwarfed those of other cities by comparison, with countless structures standing several stories tall. The city itself stretched on for a league or more. Colorful flags mounted on rooftops waved in the wind. Great flocks of birds jetted through the sky and into the city.

The closer they got, the more expansive Monarch City became. The citizens roamed freely in and out of the structured walls, some working, others playing. A band of halfling children sprinted around the wagon, holding hands, giggling, and singing before sprinting off again.

Most of the people they passed offered a smile or a greeting. The men tipped their chins or woven hats, and the women waved casually.

As they approached the edge of city, Dyphestive's back straightened, and he sniffed, his nostrils flaring. "What is that smell?" His belly groaned loudly. "It's making me salivate."

Crane's nose lifted. "Ah, that's warm butter cake, one of my favorites. There are more desserts here than you could ever imagine. My favorites have the sweet frosting slathered on." He turned his head to eye Grey Cloak and Zora. "It looks like everyone is hungry. Today, dinner is my treat."

7

The remaining members of Talon enjoyed a delicious meal on the terrace overlooking the city streets. Dyphestive sawed into his second steak, butter dripping from his chin. He wiped his forearm across his face and bit into a piece of steak big enough to choke a lion.

"Don't forget to chew before you swallow," Grey Cloak quipped.

Dyphestive gulped down the hunk of meat. "Sorry, but sometimes I'm so hungry that I forget to taste it." He washed the meat down with milk from a metal pitcher. "Oh, that's good. I haven't had milk in such a long time. Back at Dark Mountain, it was either well water or sour wine, and Scar would always make me drink the wine."

Zora, who sat between Grey Cloak and Dyphestive, put

her hand on Dyphestive's forearm. "They put you through a lot, didn't they? I'm sorry."

Dyphestive shrugged. "I'm trying not to look back, but it's not easy. I'm looking forward to my freedom."

Crane stuck his chest out and proudly said, "Monarch City is the home of the free. Did I mention that I'm from here?"

"Several times," Grey Cloak answered. His attention was on the bustling streets below. He'd noted all of the races—men, dwarves, elves, gnomes, orcs, lizardmen, halflings, gnolls, and even goblins strolled over the stones. Exotic music and dances were performed on the street corners. Acrobats made their talents known, juggling anything from knives and hatchets to glassware and eggs. The people were jovial and otherwise fantastic. "How many people to you think live here?"

"They do a census every five years. I know. I conduct them. It's a very important responsibility to the Brother-hood of Whispers," Crane said. He took a sip of wine. "The funny thing is that I'm only responsible for a section. I turn my count in to the Monarchs and never receive the final numbers. But alas, the brotherhood has a member involved in every count, and the number is over five hundred thou-sand." He winked at Zora. "But you didn't hear that from me. Besides, most people don't really know how big that number is."

Grey Cloak stared down the main road leading to a

tremendous castle positioned in the center of the city. The castle was surrounded by a wall, complete with a draw-bridge and a moat. Giant stone statues of knights that looked as real as any man encircled the castle, standing thirty feet tall. He counted a dozen statues as they passed Monarch Castle on the way in. He fed a link of sausage to Streak.

"What are you thinking?" Zora asked as she nibbled on a hunk of cheese.

"One thing is for certain: this is the perfect place to get lost. Any chance that the Doom Riders can follow us here?" Grey Cloak asked Crane.

"Not likely, at least not with the gourn. As for the members of the Scourge, well, there won't be any stopping them," Crane replied. "Try not to worry about it. It will ruin your stay, which just might be for a very long time."

Grey Cloak nodded. "Yes, I think I could get used to it here. There are so many opportunities." He lifted an eyebrow at a beautiful older woman dressed in extravagant clothing and walking two runt dragons down the street on leashes. He pulled Streak out of his hood and held the dragon where he could see the street. "Look. Kindred."

Streak remained as rigid as a board, but his pink tongue flickered out of his mouth. His body was warm in Grey Cloak's hands. "I don't suppose the people here are going to be frightened by his appearance."

"A small dragon like that? Never," Crane said. "Besides,

many people think that the runts are just lizards, and most people haven't seen a real dragon except on rare occasion." He patted his belly and yawned. "Is anyone else getting tired?"

"Who can sleep when there is so much to see?" Grey Cloak asked.

Zora had a sparkle in her eye. "I'm with you. I want to see everything. What about you, Dyphestive?"

"I'm not tired, but I wouldn't mind a long night's sleep. I can't remember the last time I had one." Dyphestive turned to Crane. "What are we supposed to do now that we're here? Are we still members of Talon? Is Talon even a group?"

As all eyes turned to Crane, he propped his elbows on the table and rested his chin on his interlocked fingers. "For now, you need stay near here. When the time comes, the Wizard Watch will find you."

"Like Dalsay used to?" Zora asked.

Crane nodded. "Very much like that. I imagine that the quest for the dragon charms is still underway and that the Sky Riders continue to build their forces. But this war behind the scenes is a battle of patience and cunning. I'll learn more in my travels, but in the meantime, it's imperative that you stay here." He slid a large emerald coin across the table. It was the medallion of location. "When the time comes, they'll find you." He pushed his chair back and stood.

"Who will find us? Tatiana?" Zora asked.

Crane shrugged. "I don't know who it might be. No one ever knows what the wizards are thinking."

"So, what are we supposed to do in the meantime?" Grey Cloak rolled the emerald medallion over his fingers.

"Do what you've always dreamed of doing. Explore. Venture. Monarch City is full of wonders far beyond what the naked eye can see." Crane covered his mouth and yawned. "Any questions?"

"Are we still Talon?" Grey Cloak asked.

"I don't see why not."

"Who is in charge?"

Crane pointed a stubby finger back at Grey Cloak. "You're asking most of the questions, so I'd venture to say that you are. All in favor say 'Aye.'"

"Aye," Dyphestive, Zora, and Crane said simultaneously.

"It seems the ayes have it." Crane smiled. He set the location box down on the table. "Make the most of it."

8

GUNDER ISLAND

The Lords of the Air gathered inside the great halls of Hidemark, a sanctuary buried inside the crater of Gunder Island. The lords, also known as Sky Riders, sat around an oval table, their faces tense. Among them were Justus, Anya's uncle, Yuri Gnomeknower, a wizened woman with deep eyes full of knowledge, the big-bellied dwarf Hammerjaw, Slomander, the lizardman, Hogrim, an orc with a head as big as a bull, and the elven brother, Aric, and his two sisters, Stayzie and Mayzie, each elegant and strikingly beautiful.

Justus broke the silence with an audible sigh. He rose up from his seat and spoke. "I know that all of you are angry about Anya's actions. Her aiding Grey Cloak left no doubt that she has betrayed us all. I promise you, she will be punished when she returns."

Hammerjaw came to his feet and slammed his fists on the stone table. "*If* she returns! Stop protecting her, Justus. I understand she is kin, but we must track her down. Stop delaying. You are wasting valuable time." He pounded his fist. "Delay! Delay! Delay!"

"I'm still in charge," Justus said calmly. "We wait."

"We delay!" Hammerjaw insisted.

"I know my niece. She will return. All of you know this. Not a single one of us has ever doubted her before. And what are we angry about, that she freed an elf, a legacy, that we were going to imprison?" Justus flicked his hands. "None of it is right in our eyes, but in her heart, it must have been. We have to trust our brethren. She'll be back."

"I, for one, insist that we go after her," Hammerjaw pressed, "and I am not alone."

"Agreed," Hogrim said.

Aric and his sisters nodded as well.

Justus pointed at the lot of them. "One Sky Rider on the loose is dangerous enough, let alone sending out four more. Do I have to remind you again that Anya battled Riskers on the edges of Lake Flugen? How close must our enemy be before you see them?" He paced behind his chair. "We have twelve apprenti in training to be riders, dragons that are growing. Our army is building, and we need to stay on course, not traipse off on some adventure." His voice softened. "And for that matter, Hammerjaw, did you even once stop to consider that perhaps Anya and Cinder are in danger? It's been a long time. They could have perished or been captured, for all we know."

Hammerjaw's face tucked deeper behind his beard as he mumbled, "It's a matter of principle."

Yuri climbed onto the tabletop and tapped her foot. "I agree with Justus. We are at a junction where it is more important to look ahead than it is behind. Sadly, we don't know the fate of Anya, or Grey Cloak, for that matter. We can only hope that they safely return to our midst because in my gut, I feel that we need them. As for the apprenti, I am pleased to report that they are all excelling during their ripening. They are eager. They are loyal. They are hungry. Let us focus our attention on what we have, not what we have lost."

"Thank you, Yuri," Justus said as he eased into his chair. "Your wisdom is without rival at this table. Can we please set our differences aside and focus on the future before it is lost?"

Murmurs stirred among the group.

Hammerjaw, who was whispering with Hogrim, spoke up. "We demand a vote for a new leader of the Lords of the Air. If you win the majority, we'll keep with your plan."

Justus rolled his eyes. "Again, you bring this up, and I tell you, it is not my time."

"No, but if you agree to it, it can be," Hammerjaw

argued. "Let us decide whether or not we want to follow your direction."

"All of this because you want to chase down Anya?"

"No, all of this because you are not a strong leader, and the likes of Anya take advantage of it. It leaves the apprenti with a bad impression. We hear them talking about it when our backs are turned and they don't think we're listening," Hammerjaw replied. "Your time has come, Justus. Now, let us decide who is best to lead us into tomorrow and beyond."

In all their days of bickering back and forth on the same topic, that was the first time Hammerjaw made a succinct point. Justus had overheard the apprenti talking about Anya's situation. It wasn't a matter that could be kept secret, but it made an impression, and worst of all, it created doubt. For once, Justus agreed. Hammerjaw was right. The Sky Riders needed a leader who left no doubts about their character.

I can't believe I'm going along with this.

Hammerjaw crossed his arms over his barrel chest and beard. "Well?"

Everyone at the table fixed their eyes on Justus.

He opened his mouth to speak.

A hard knock came from the door. It sounded frantic. "Lords! Lords!" one of the apprenti called from outside. "Come quick!"

Stayzie was the first to the door, and she flung it open.

A young elf waited on the other side. His face was beady with sweat, and his eyes were bigger than saucers.

"What is wrong?" Stayzie asked.

"Dragons! I've never seen so many," the young elf panted. "They gather above the crater."

9

Just below the sunlit clouds above Hidemark's crater, a thunder of dragons circled. Justus counted twenty middling dragons, four grand dragons, and another score of the drake. He ground his teeth. The sanctuary of Hidemark was lost.

"Gather the dragons, everyone," Justus said, "but stay on the ground. We need to fully understand what this is."

"It's war. That's what this is," Hogrim said. The battle-ready orc buckled metal bracers over his bulging forearms and jammed his dragon-rider helm on his head. "It's time to fight."

"No one is fighting anyone," Justus said as he buckled on his sword belt. "At least not yet. We'll wait and see what they want."

"The longer we delay, the greater their force will

become," Hammerjaw said as a middling dragon crawled out of the woodland to his side. While he waited, two elven apprenti hurried over with his dragon's saddle and buckled it on. He climbed into the saddle and, with his hands, charged his thunder javelins with glowing energy. "We should strike now."

"Don't be absurd." Yuri Gnomeknower, dressed in a full suit of plate armor, put her fingers to her lips and whistled. Another middling dragon crawled out of the woods with its head low. The dragon curled around her body while the apprenti geared it. "As long as we stay on the ground, we're safe. If we take to the skies, we'll be doomed."

One by one, dragons snaked out of the forest. In a rush of feet, the apprenti made quick work of equipping every dragon with saddles. Only Hammerjaw and Yuri rode the middlings. Hogrim, Slomander, Aric, Mayzie, and Stayzie loaded onto their grands.

Justus quickly climbed onto Firestok. "Are the fledglings safe?" he asked her.

Firestok nodded. "Lethas Lagoon is the safest possible place." She eyed the sky. "There are many, and they've come to fight. I hear them crowing like demons, taunting us."

Justus petted her neck. "Well, they will have to bring the fight to us. Let them posture all they want." He stood up in his stirrups. "Listen, Sky Riders! Listen, apprenti! We are on giant ground. If they want to fight us, they will have to land. And if they land, not only will they fight us, they will fight the giants as well. Believe me when I say the giants loathe Black Frost and his minions."

"I want to ride the sky!" Hammerjaw barked. "How do you know the giants will fight with us? They are far from a reliable sort."

As if on command, the treetops shook and the ground quaked. The distant sound of a giant's footsteps followed. *Thoom. Thoom. Thoom. Thoom. Thoom.* Branches snapped loudly, and birds scattered into the air as a great bulk moved among the trees. A giant emerged, pushing his face through the tallest branches of the trees. The Sky Riders' eyes lifted upward.

The giant towered over thirty feet tall. His head was bald, but his body was covered in shaggy hair. He had heavy eyes and an aggravated look on his face. "Justus, who are those that fly above?" He spoke in a loud and rumbling voice. "Are they yours?"

"No, Garthar!" Justus answered at the top of his lungs to ensure his voice reached the giant's long ears. "Those are Riskers, minions of Black Frost! They've come for us!"

Garthar rubbed his mouth. "Hmmm... I thought so. If Black Frost's children touch so much as a talon on giant ground, they will die!" He punched his fist into his hand with a loud *smack*, creating a gust of wind. "My brothers and I will crush them. We will crush them all!" He moved his huge body back between the branches and disappeared into the trees.

Thoom. Thoom. Thoom. Garthar's retreat faded, and he was gone.

"Does that answer your question?" Mayzie smugly asked Hammerjaw.

"We'll see what happens when the fighting starts. Until then, seeing is believing."

As the apprenti armored up and grabbed weaponry for ground battle, all eyes remained fixed on the sky.

Black Frost's forces were growing, like bees swarming out of a hive. Over the next hour, the Sky Riders watched the sky above. Four grands became twelve. Twelve middlings became thirty-six. The drakes were so many, they couldn't be counted.

Justus put his helmet on and buckled the chin strap. Hot blood coursed through his veins. "If this is our final battle, let it be our finest battle."

10

"There are so many," Firestok said to Justus. The dragon's gaze was cast upward, and her voice had a hint of worry. "So many of them were our friends. Now, they come to kill us."

"Or enslave us." Justus finished charging his thunder javelins and buckled his helmet. "Either way, we will not yield. They would be fools to fight us on the ground. The giants are many as well."

"I see a banner of negotiation descending from the clouds," Aric said. The elven Sky Rider sat atop a grand dragon, Codius, who had the same dark-toned scales and colorful markings as Firestok but were green instead of orange. "Shall I parley? I see three of them."

"We'll both go," Justus said. "Everyone else, wait here." He patted Firestok on the neck. "Ride the sky!"

Justus and Aric's dragons spread their great wings as their powerful rear legs launched them skyward.

Three Riskers on grands circled far below the sky army. They were led by a soldier in full black plate armor and a dragon-fashioned helm. In hand, he carried an orange-and-blue banner of negotiation. Two young blond warriors flew behind him, a man and a woman. All three were equipped with bows, and quivers full of arrows hung from their dragons' saddles.

Justus recognized the leader immediately as Commander Shaw. His tall, lean frame was a dead give-away. The much younger pair, he did not know. He and Aric joined the enemy to fly in a tight aerial ring.

"It's been a very long time, Justus," Commander Shaw said haughtily. "You appear well."

"You still carry the sneering countenance of a traitor. Even from here you stink of it," Justus replied.

"You sound bitter, my old friend. But there is no need for that." Commander Shaw looked casually Aric's way. "It's good to see you as well, Aric. You appear more radiant than Justus, but at our age, most elves do."

"I wish I could say the same of you, but if I did, I'd be lying," Aric responded. "Your heart is still wrought with evil. Even with your armor on, I can see it. Who are these children you brought with you? Are they the spawn of you and your dear Adalia?"

"This is Dirklen and Magnolia. They are naturals, but

I'm sure you can assess that already. After all, they are perfect, are they not?" Commander Shaw asked.

Dirklen had flowing blond hair that spilled out from underneath his helmet, and he wore a sneer. Magnolia, his twin, had curly hair but was wide-eyed and curious. A deviousness hid deep in her eyes, as if she were a cat preparing to pounce on its prey.

Justus scowled. "You carry the banner of negotiation, so let's hear what you have to say. I have no desire to get acquainted with your evil brood."

With a gloating look, Commander Shaw spoke over the wind. "The terms of the negotiation are simple. I'm certain that you recall Black Frost's final words before you betrayed him."

"Of course I remember. How could I forget his words on the Day of Betrayal? 'Join me or die,'" Justus replied. "Is he making the same generous offer again? What a surprise."

"Don't be a fool, Justus. You might have slipped through Black Frost's claws last time, but I assure you, it won't happen again." Commander Shaw glanced up. "Look about. We have superior numbers, and no matter which direction you and the Sky Riders flee, there will be no escape."

"We escaped the last time," Justus said.

"Quit chatting with this old fool, and let us kill him," Dirklen said. He sat tall in his saddle and pushed his chest out. "We are wasting our breath. Let's annihilate him."

"Curb your tongue, Dirklen!" Commander Shaw ordered. "Justus, I apologize for his brash tongue. He is young and very eager. Do you have an answer to Black Frost's offer?"

"Let me hear you officially make that offer."

"In Black Frost's very own words, 'Join me or die.'"

"Tell Black Frost that he can take his offer and shove it up your dragon's behind." He glanced at Dirklen. "Or his."

Commander Shaw's face darkened. "You are a fool. Today, all of you will die."

"We'll see. And I think the giants might have something to say about that as well. Why don't you come down and extend that same offer to them?" He glanced above. "Better yet, why doesn't Black Frost do it personally? I'm sure that Garthar would love to see him. Where is your leader? Does he still hide in the shadows of Dark Mountain?"

"Blasphemer!" Dirklen notched an arrow and aimed it at Justus. "You will pay!"

"Put that bow away, you fool! This is not how Riskers conduct themselves!" Commander Shaw said. "Justus, share my offer with the others. I'll give you time. It's the least I can do before you all die." He pulled his dragon's reins and led the twins higher into the sky to join the others.

Dirklen glared at Justus as they flew away.

Justus casually waved.

"I think you gave them more fire for the battle," Aric quipped.

"Would you have handled it another way?"

"No, I'm glad you whizzed on their boots. I've said the same, if not worse." Aric eyeballed the enemy. "I know our chances are slim, but I hope we kill those two men. They have it coming."

Justus nodded and patted his sword. "Agreed. I'll take Shaw's head, and you take Dirklen's, if they don't burn first."

11

With the Sky Riders gathered in front of Hidemark's temple entrance, Hammerjaw said, "What did our dear friend, Commander Shaw, have to say?"

"The same as always: surrender or die," Aric said as he removed his helmet. "One would think that Black Frost could come up with another line. If it were me, I think I'd use 'Join me or die.' That has more panache."

Stayzie and Mayzie managed a pair of nervous laughs.

"The timing of your dry wit is as inappropriate as ever," Stayzie said. She covered her full head of hair with her helmet. "Just, if the Riskers come down, what are your orders? Are we fighting as teams or going it alone?"

Justus considered his options. He had no idea what sort of action the giants might take. Their methods were unpredictable. Splitting up the Sky Riders would only expose a single rider. If Commander Shaw brought all of his forces down on them, they had only one logical move to make. "As one, we stand together to the end."

"There's not going to be an end. Not this day!" Hammerjaw bellowed.

Hogrim beat his chest with his fist. "Let them come. Hogrim will destroy them all."

"As much as it might kill them, make sure your dragons stay on the ground. The Riskers will do anything they can to bait us into the sky," Justus said. "That's what they want. We will stay our ground and bring them to us. It will be an even match, so long as we stand with the giants."

"Let them come and taste the dragon flame!" Slomander hissed. He shook his fist in the sky. "Let them come!"

Yuri rode her middle dragon over to Justus and Firestok. She looked like a child on a small pony by comparison. "Do we even know how many giant allies we have? There are scores of them up there."

Justus cracked his neck side to side. "It doesn't make a difference now. The only thing that matters is that we take as many as we can and hope we break their will."

"And then?"

"And then we'll have to find another place to hide and hope all of us are still alive."

"My bones ache, and my heart twists," Yuri said. "I feel

a growing sense of dread. I fear, despite our efforts, that we won't all make it."

"I think we all feel the same," Justus said. "That's why we can't let them win." He turned Firestok around and faced everyone. He cleared his dry throat. "I want you all to know that I have been honored to be your leader since the Day of Betrayal. We have been on the run ever since, but we all knew that this day would come. We are well prepared for it. This is the moment we live for, train for, fight for, and die for. All of the world depends on us because, if we fail, Gapoli will be lost to the forces of darkness forever.

"If you see dragon charms, aim for them. The Riskers will lose control of their dragons. Only a few of them will be naturals. Now is not the time for mercy. We cannot spare our enemies. We must assume they are all lost to the cause of evil.

"As your leader, my sole regret is that it has come to this. If only we could have struck the heart of Black Frost sooner, we could have avoided this calamity. But there is hope." Justus's voice rose and strengthened. "There is always hope for the brave. We fight with purpose. We fight with cause. With passion. With heart. With honor. Our battle is just, and we are righteous!

"Today they will hear the roar of our dragons and hear the songs of our swords. We are the Lords of the Air. We ride the dragons' flames. We are the Sky Riders. Victory is our destiny!" He pulled his sword. "Our victory will be their curse!"

Every Sky Rider and apprentice lifted a gleaming dragon blade in salute.

"Ride, Sky Riders!" Hammerjaw said.

"Fly, Sky Riders!" Yuri elated.

"Fight, Sky Riders!" Hogrim shouted.

"To thunderbolts, fire, and victory!" Aric pumped his sword in the air. His eyes glowed with inner fire. He turned them toward the enemy. "Come, you filthy lizards, come! We are ready!"

Justus's blood turned hot. The wizardry he channeled coursed through his veins. He was ready. They all were. He had one more thing to say as he watched the first wave of enemies descend. "Destroy, Sky Riders! Destroy!"

A train of drakes, over twenty in number, plunged. They were much like middling dragons but riderless and sleeker. Unlike full-blooded dragons, which had front legs and paws, they only had smaller handlike claws on the edges of their wings. They dove through the sky, their long snouts open and shrieking. They aimed their scaled, serpentine bodies toward the Sky Riders.

The Gunder giants' massive heads popped up among the trees. In their monstrous hands, they carried huge slings and stones. The stones whistled over the Sky Riders' heads and rocketed skyward.

The front line of drakes split away, the second rank

taking the blast full force. Solid rock collided with flesh, and resounding cracks of splintering bones carried over the valley. Drakes dropped from the sky and crashed into the trees. The moment they landed, the woodland shook from the scramble of giants. They stomped the drakes underfoot and tore the wings from their backs.

Giants reloaded their slings as others hurled wood and round stones.

The train of drakes scattered, their aerial prowess nimble, as this time they were prepared. They evaded, regrouped, and came down on the Sky Riders with hate burning in their eyes.

12

"Strike, Sky Riders! Strike!" Justus commanded.

From the back of their dragons, the Sky Riders unleashed their thunder javelins. Each and every one of the missiles sailed true and ripped into the drakes' ranks. The javelins tore through wings, impaled bodies, and exploded with thunderous effect.

Many Drakes snaked away from the aerial assault, twisting through the air and attacking the Sky Riders from the side. One of the trio dove at Justus and Firestok. It landed on Firestok's face and dug its talons into her scales.

Justus stabbed the drake with his sword just below its wing. Its barbed tail struck like a scorpion's, punching into his chest armor. The barb, dripping with poison, snapped off the end of its tail. Dropplets of poison sprayed and burned the skin on Justus's face. He let out a painful "gah!" Small red boils rose on his skin.

The drake shrieked at Justus, the scales on its neck flaring out like a shield. Justus stabbed his dragon sword into its side. The drake let out another piercing shriek.

Firestok bit into the drake's tail. With her claws, she ripped the drake from her face and slammed it on the ground. She put her full weight on the drake's writhing body and crushed it underneath her talons.

The fighting on the ground became a furious frenzy. Angry knots of drakes pounced on the dragons and their riders.

"Fight, Sky Riders! Fight!" Justus called out.

Hogrim stood on top of his dragon's saddle, swinging a two-handed dragon sword with fury. *Slice!* He took a drake's head clean off as it flew by.

"Die, drake, die!" Hammerjaw roared from the seat of his saddle. His middling dragon was locked in mortal combat with one drake while he battled for his life against another. A drake clamped its jaws over the dwarf's arm. Hammerjaw plunged his dragon sword hilt-deep into the drake's heart.

The drake's jaws opened as it fell to the ground. Hammerjaw's arm was covered with dragon armor, but fresh blood shined on the metal.

"Hammerjaw, is the wound grave?" Justus shouted.

"Hah!" Hammerjaw said in a mighty voice. "But a

scratch and a wake-up call. Bring on more of the winged lizards. I shall kill them all!"

Hammerjaw's middling dragon bit into a drake's neck and broke it with a snap as loud as breaking timber. It shook the drake like an angry dog and flung it away.

A drake soared toward Stayzie from behind. Mayzie blasted the dragon with a thunder javelin. The drake's body puffed out from the explosion. It twisted in the air, hit the ground, and skipped against a giant's toes. The giant picked the drake up like it was a dead varmint and hurled it at another drake.

As one, the Sky Riders, dragons, and Gunder giants threw their bodies against the vicious force of drakes.

Aric stood on the ground, a thunder javelin glowing like fire in his hand, and met a drake's charge. He hit the drake in the chest just as the drake bowled him over. They tumbled, one rolling over the other, until Aric landed on top and pushed the javelin deeper into the drake's chest. The fire in the javelin's shaft flashed. The drake's body exploded, smoke rolling out of its mouth and nose.

Slomander's grand dragon, Rodfire, pinned a drake's tail under one of his mighty paws, stretched his jaws open, and let out a stream of flames. The intense heat of the dragon's breath charred the shrieking drake's scales. Its body shrank as it baked, the juices of life in its body drying up. Its skin and scales crackled as it turned into a burning husk.

The foul stench of scorched scales and fallen foes carried across the valley. Life in the forest scattered as the battle raged.

Garthar the giant carried two dead drakes by the neck. He held them to the sky like trophies. "More! Bring us more!"

The first wave of the enemy was routed. The drake they didn't kill fled back into the sky.

The Sky Riders and their apprenti cheered.

"Victory, Sky Riders! Victory!" Hammerjaw shouted.

The warriors pumped their swords and fists in the air. They hollered at the top of their lungs.

Even the giants chanted and beat their chests. They tossed drake skulls over the treetops. One of the giants drop-kicked a drake and sent if flying thirty yards away. The giants bumped chests and elbows as they grunted at one another.

Justus remained silent. He watched the Riskers' forces circle high above.

Yuri came alongside him. "This is only the beginning."

"Aye. The drakes are only shock troops, sent to reveal our strength," he said. "Commander Shaw knows our numbers now. He'll send a more powerful force next." He looked down at Yuri. "Do you still feel the same sense of dread?"

The gnome's wide eyes were on the sky. "No. I feel fire in my veins."

"Let them come, then. We are ready." He turned his attention to Garthar and shouted, "Garthar! Soon, the second wave comes! Are your people ready?"

Garthar glanced at the dragons he held in each hand. "What do you think?"

13

"What are they waiting for?" Hammerjaw demanded. He paced around his dragon with his sword in one hand and a javelin in the other. "It's been hours since they attacked."

Justus's blood had long cooled. He knew he wasn't alone either. He could see the tense, disappointed expressions on everyone's faces. Dusk had come, and the enemy remained circling in the sky. The giants had retreated into the woods.

"Commander Shaw wants to draw us out," he said. "I'd do the same. Get the enemy's juices up and bring them back down again." He huffed through his nose. "He'll attack again soon. He's not that patient, and his dragons can't circle all night."

"I believe they might be rotating with more forces waiting on the beaches," Stayzie suggested.

"I don't know about that. Across the lake, perhaps, but not on Gunder. The giants would attack them." Justus rubbed his eyes. The wait had dragged on since the start. He'd been sure the battle would remain in full swing once it started, but it had not been so. Commander Shaw was toying with him. Justus ground his teeth. "If anyone wants to rest, rest. We will set up watch in the meantime."

"Sleep? At a time like this?" Hammerjaw scoffed. "Never." He patted his stomach. "I wouldn't mind eating something. A dwarf needs his strength. Apprenti! Fetch the rations!"

Together, the Sky Riders ate a quiet meal made of dried meat and bread dipped in honey. Every man and woman was on full alert. None of them would sleep, not even when they ordered the apprenti to.

Hammerjaw did most of the talking. "This is war. There is no rest in war, only victory or death," he told the apprenti. "Dying in battle to save the lives of our brethren is the highest honor. No matter the outcome. Know this, and be proud. You stood against evil this day. What matters most is that you stood. When one stands against evil, it makes all the difference. Fight your hearts out, even when you're trembling with fear. It's far better to die trying than to do nothing at all."

The apprenti soaked up every word as they nibbled on

their meal. They might be young, but they were brave and ready. Not one of them had cowered in battle. They had held their own and fought like soldiers.

Justus took a tug of water from a canteen and corked it. The sweat and grit of battle had long dried on his face. A thousand feet above him, he could see the glow of dragon charms hanging from the necks of his enemies. They had the faint twinkle of starlight. His enemy had strength in numbers, but there was a difference between his Sky Riders and the Riskers. The Sky Riders were naturals, but not all of the Riskers were. It gave the Sky Riders an advantage. One-on-one, they were a match in skill and strength, but the Sky Riders' abilities were abnormal. They could draw magic, summon wizardry, and use it as a weapon with devastating effect. Still, he wasn't sure it would be enough.

The sky above rumbled. Everyone tilted their heads skyward, and those who weren't standing rose to their feet. The Riskers began a slow downward spiral. The quiet forest awakened as the giants pushed their way through the trees. The grand dragons in the sky huffed out bright-red-and-orange flames.

"They're coming." Justus climbed onto Firestok's back. "Everyone in formation in front of the temple entrance. Make them bring the fight to us. Fight, Sky Riders! Fight!"

The Riskers' circle of death descended faster. From one thousand feet, they dropped to five hundred, four hundred, three hundred, two hundred.

"They ready their bows!" Hammerjaw hollered. "Shields!"

The Sky Riders grabbed small round metal bucklers from their dragons' saddles.

The Riskers notched their arrows. Radiant yellow-green energy emanated from the arrows' tips. They pulled back their bowstrings and fired.

"Incoming!" Hammerjaw hollered. He didn't budge or lift his shield. "Let the celebration begin!"

The arrows streaked through the air like bright missiles. The Sky Riders covered themselves with their shields. A rapid *boom-boom-boom-boom-boom* exploded from one end of the forest to the other. The glowing missiles struck dragons and shields and exploded.

Justus caught the full force of an arrow on his shield. The bright explosion jarred his body inside his armor. "Hold your position! They fire one volley at a time! They need to reload."

Yuri's middling dragon caught an arrow between its chest scales. The arrow exploded, leaving a dark patch of smoking flesh. The dragon twisted in a circle and tried to jump into the sky.

"Yield! Rokan! Yield! We fight on the ground tonight!" Yuri said.

The Riskers' dragons split into two separate circles. The warriors on the middling dragons reloaded with arrows from their quivers. The grand dragon riders grazed the tops of the trees and spewed flames from their mouths.

The giants rose up in the woodland, hurling trees like javelins, only to see the graceful beasts of the air gliding away.

"Incoming!" Justus shouted.

The second volley of arrows rocketed toward them. The missiles exploded into man and beast.

An arrow knocked Aric out of his saddle. Carried down by his heavy armor, he crashed into the ground.

Firestok took an arrow in one of her horns. It exploded and rocked her head backward, bucking Justus in the saddle.

He held on. "Easy, Firestok!"

"Those arrows have the sting of fire in them!" Firestok replied. "We can't sit on the ground and take this. Let me spread my wings and take to the air."

"No. They must come to us. They will come to us." He lifted his voice. "All of us together. Stand your ground! They can't cower in the skies forever!"

The trees burned. Smoke plumes darkened the skies. The voices of angry giants shook the ground.

With chaos erupting from all directions, Justus hollered once more, "Incoming!"

14

The forest burned, and giants fought among the flames. The entire area in front of the temple had become a war zone.

A grand dragon grazed the treetops, flames spewing from its mouth. A giant jumped into the sky, wrapped his mighty arms around the dragon's neck, and pulled it to the ground. The titans wrestled among the trees. The dragon coiled its tail around the giant's neck, its hot breath burning into the giant's flesh. The giant roared as it bashed a stone against the dragon's skull and knocked the Risker out of the saddle.

Justus caught the battle out of the corner of his eye as another wave of Riskers on middling dragons flew overhead. They fired another volley of glowing arrows that streaked through the night like shooting stars.

Jarring explosions erupted all around. Dragons roared, and fighters screamed. Justus caught another arrow on his buckler and absorbed the explosion. He teetered in the saddle. "Stay your positions! Stay your positions!"

The aerial assault seesawed back and forth for hours. The Riskers were content to pick away at the Sky Riders from a distance, but they weren't doing any real harm. The giants hurled tremendous boulders and logs with devastating effect. The huge missiles knocked riders from their saddles on more than one occasion, and the smaller middling dragons crashed to the ground and were pummeled to death.

"Fight, you cowards! Fight us!" Hammerjaw yelled as he launched a thunder javelin into the breast of a middling dragon that flew too low. The missile exploded. The dragon bucked in the air, tossing its rider, and it barrel-rolled into the ground. "Hah! Mighty thunderbolts! I've downed another!"

The dragons' fiery breaths licked up the woodland like kindling, creating walls of flames. Smoking trees fell, and the fires rose higher.

Justus wiped sweat from his eyes. He was cooking like a dead fish laid out in the sun. The heat was suffocating.

"This is going to go on forever," Yuri said, blocking an arrow with a small round mystic shield that she procured for herself. "Surely they don't think we can be defeated like this."

Justus searched the sky. High above, he could make out Commander Shaw, Dirklen, and Magnolia circling above the battling ranks. "Shaw is no fool. He's only probing for a weakness."

All of a sudden, a pair of grand dragons dropped away from the train and snatched a giant from the field of fire. With their talons locked around the giant's arms, they lifted him, thrashing and yelling, into the air. Climbing to new heights, the dragons flew over the Sky Riders and dropped the giant.

"Oh no!" Justus's eyes widened. He pointed at the falling giant. "Incoming! Move, everyone, move!"

The plummeting giant landed back-first on the ground.

Whomp!

The Sky Riders scattered just in time. All eyes were on the giant. The huge man was dead, and his body sunk into the ground.

"Well, that's one way to leave an impression," Hogrim quipped. He stuck his chin out and eyed the sky. "Cowards!"

The giants inside the flaming forest came to life. With loud howls and grunts, they hurled boulders and logs like men gone wild.

A log spun end over end and crushed a middling rider in his saddle. The glowing dragon charm on the man's chest fell off as he plummeted toward the earth. As the man tumbled, a giant batted him with a club, launching him across the forest.

"I bet he felt that one." Hammerjaw watched as the Risker sailed through the air and into the flames.

For another hour, the Riskers played the same game. They picked on the giants and Sky Riders, but they had little effect. The Sky Riders and dragons held their ground as they helped the giants take down a small Risker from time to time.

Justus was getting sick of the deadlock. It was time to send a message. "Sky Riders, lend me your ears! When the next wave of grands flies over, we all will launch our thunder javelins at the grand behind the leader. We will knock that lizard from the sky and let the giants feast on him. Are you with me?"

"Aye! Aye! Aye!" the Sky Riders shouted. They all filled their hands with glowing javelins.

The next wave of dragons dove down and passed overhead.

With his javelin cocked over his shoulder, Justus shouted, "Unleash the thunderbolts!"

Every Sky Rider flung their javelin with perfect accuracy. The radiant missiles rocketed upward, seeming to gain speed as they flew.

The lead grand dragon bent away from the barrage of javelins. The second grand dragon began its turn, but the Sky Riders timed it perfectly. The grand dragon turned right into the javelins' paths. Every javelin exploded into the dragon's body.

A series of loud pops followed the strike. The dragon let out a pained and angry roar. Its wings beat desperately as it tried to lift its smoking and damaged body. Its strength fled, and its wings collapsed behind its back. It dropped right in front of them with a resounding *thud*.

A Risker in black plate-mail armor jumped out of the wounded dragon's saddle, his sword in hand. His lithe body moved like a cat. He set his eyes on the Sky Riders and beckoned them with his sword. "We meet again, brothers and sisters," he gloated. "Which one of you wants to die first?" He pointed a finger at the apprenti. "How about them? They are going to die anyway. All of you are."

15

"Bergamo Taug," Justus said to the man who fell from the sky. "I'll ask you once to drop your sword and surrender."

"Hah," Bergamo said with a cocky grin. He stroked his long moustache then unbuckled his dragon helm and cast it aside. "You know that won't happen, Justus. You should have surrendered when you had the chance. Now, I challenge you, any of you, blade against blade. I'm tired of flying, and I'm ready to do some real fighting." He scanned their faces. "Who will it be?" He pointed his sword at Mayzie. "How about you, pretty lady? What was your name again? Sorry, but I can't remember them all."

"That's because you're stupid," Mayzie said as she climbed down from her dragon's saddle. Her sword glowed bright blue and shined like the sun as she channeled her wizardry into it. "And you know what they say about stupid people. You live stupid and you die stupid."

Bergamo sneered. "We'll see who's stupid." His sword shined. He made a gentle bow. "Shall we dance?"

"I'll dance," Mayzie said. "You'll die." She leapt into the air as if her feet had wings. Her body twisted in a full arc, and she struck. Her sword crashed against Bergamo's, and she had him parrying for his life and shuffling backward.

Justus's jaw tightened. His hand squeezed the handle of his sword. He knew he wasn't alone in wanting to help Mayzie. All of the Sky Riders did. And he knew Bergamo. He was a seasoned fighter, older and crafty, who knew every trick in the book. But dragon riders lived by a code. Bergamo made the challenge. Mayzie accepted. No one could interfere. Justus only hoped she could handle herself against one of the best, for he'd never seen her fight before.

With every eye fixed on the duel, Firestok twisted her head around to look at Justus. "They land."

"What?" Justus tore his eyes from the melee. The Riskers and their dragons dropped to the ground in packs made up of one grand and three middlings. They ganged up on single giants and attacked.

The huge men tangled with the serpentine strength of the dragons. The dragons gushed waves of flames, but the thick-skinned giants fought through the scorching flames, hammering the dragons' scaly bodies with their fists.

Riskers fired an onslaught of arrows into the giants. The

arrows exploded in their massive bodies, but the huge men didn't slow. They chased down the Riskers, snatched them up, and pounded them into the ground.

Before Justus's eyes, Garthar locked into mortal combat with a full-grown grand dragon, his rider, and a brood of middlings. Flames gushed from the grand dragon's mouth, scorching the coarse hair on the giant's hide. Garthar put the dragon in a headlock and twisted. The forest floor quaked as the dragon's body smashed burning trees. With middling dragons latched onto Garthar's legs, the dragons' riders striking him with swords and arrows, Garthar punched the grand dragon in the face. Dragon claws raked over the giant's body and ripped open his flesh. The thirty-foot-tall titan increased the pressure on the dragon's neck. His muscles bulged, and his chest heaved. The grand dragon choked out its last flame, and a moment later, its neck snapped.

The Risker riding the grand dragon climbed up Garthar's back and stabbed deep into the giant's neck with a shimmering sword. Garthar's eyes popped open wide. He sank to a knee and moaned. His arms dropped. The Risker let out a triumphant shout and pumped his fist in the air.

A crafty look appeared in Garthar's eyes. With startling quickness, Garthar plucked the Risker from his back and grasped him in the palm of his hand. "You can't kill me, flea!" Using two hands, Garthar crushed the Risker like a walnut in a nutcracker. He peeled the middlings away from his body and slammed them together. Their riders fled into the forest.

Justus turned his focus back to Mayzie and Bergamo. Bergamo's right shoulder drooped, and his right hand was missing. He parried desperately with his left hand. Cool as the wind, Mayzie batted the Risker's weapon out of his grip and slid her sword into his exposed body. Bergamo died with the Sky Riders cheering all around him.

The Sky Riders and the giants were standing strong, and Justus knew the battle wouldn't last forever. The Riskers had over a score of middlings and at least a dozen grands. But their number was dwindling, and the giants had only lost a few.

Garthar pulled the sword free from his neck and flicked it away. He cast his heavy eyes toward Justus. "We will beat them." He beat his chest. "We will kill all of them." He stuck his wounded leg in the flames of a burning tree. "Their fire is hot but not hot enough to harm us." The skin around his wound mended. "The Gunder giants are indestructible." He beat his chest several more times. "Hoh! Hoh! Hoh! Brothers, dragon flesh will fill our bellies tonight, tomorrow, and forever more!"

The Riskers on the ground broke off their attack and launched back into the sky. They joined with the thunder of dragons in the air, who calmly circled above the battleground.

The Sky Riders and giants cheered, swinging their arms and taunting the enemy.

Justus could feel Commander Shaw's eyes on him. He rubbed the side of his cheek. "We've wounded them." He glanced at Bergamo's corpse lying on the ground. He was surprised Mayzie had killed the warrior so easily. "Well done, sister."

She wiped her blade off on a cloth and sheathed it. She winced as she did so, covering a bloody spot on the side of her armor. "He gouged me good. I had to finish him quick or die. It's amazing what the threat of death can do."

"Aye."

"Justus, look." Yuri pointed at the sky.

The Riskers flew low and poured bags of sand from their saddles. The sand sparkled, made a fine mist, and spread out over the burning wood. It clung to everything it touched.

"What is it?" Hammerjaw asked as he picked a fleck from his arm. "Is it snow?"

Inside the burning forest, the giants started to collapse. Garthar swayed and rubbed his eyes as the flakes clung to his body. He pitched backward like a felled tree.

Thump!

Yuri gasped after tasting one of the flakes. "It's giant's bane."

Justus looked up as the enemy landed again.

16

The Sky Riders formed a defensive half circle in front of Hidemark's temple entrance. The apprenti gathered behind them.

Commander Shaw sat on the back of his dragon in front of a host of Riskers, Dirklen and Magnolia at his sides. All three of them rode grand dragons. Many more grands and middling dragons stood behind them, over a score in all. Trains of middlings and drakes circled above, poised to strike down any dragon that tried to escape.

"This is the end, Justus," Commander Shaw said. "The giants are down, and we have superior numbers. Surrender, and I'll make your execution quick and painless."

"There won't be a surrender today, Shaw," Justus said. "And the giant's bane won't keep the Gunder down for long. We'll be happy to thin out your brood between now and then." He patted the flat of his sword on Firestok's horns. "But if you'd like, the two of us can settle this."

"Bold words from a man who is about to face annihilation," Commander Shaw said. "Of course, if I weren't under orders, I would gladly accept your challenge."

"You are a coward, Shaw."

"No, I'm a survivor." Commander Shaw tipped is head upward. "Look around you, all of you. Our ranks are growing by the day. We have the dragon charms, naturals, and more apprenti in our army. Day by day, Black Frost's forces become bigger while yours grow smaller." His eyes slid over the Sky Riders' apprenti. "Ah, but I do see new apprenti. I will spare them if they pledge their loyalty to Black Frost."

"Never!" one of the young male elves shouted from the ranks of the apprenti.

"We aren't going to lose, Shaw." Justus knitted his brow.

"You sound so sure of yourself," Commander Shaw replied.

"He reeks of fear and babbles like a fool," Dirklen added.

"Boy, I can't wait to wipe that smug look off your face, but in the meantime, let me tell you why you will lose," Justus said.

Dirklen snorted. "Humor me, you old goat."

"You see, boy, the likes of you and all of them"—he poked his finger at the Riskers—"have no spines. That is your legacy. When Black Frost rose up, rather than fight and resist, they aligned with the cowardice that filled their own black hearts. Look at them, your naturals and dragon riders with great gifts—when the time came to use those gifts, their weak spirits broke."

"It wasn't us—the Sky Riders, the Lords of the Air— that lost that day. It was you, Commander Shaw. All you bootlicking cowards lost the moment you caved. You've been lost ever since. You will be, so long as you stay on the wrong side of right."

Commander Shaw's long face sagged toward his chest.

Dirklen started a hollow clap.

Magnolia giggled goofily.

"That's quite the speech for a dead man," Dirklen mocked. "What a shame none of you will survive long enough to remember it." He gave Commander Shaw a bored look. "We've talked long enough. It's time to kill them now."

"Agreed." Commander Shaw lifted his arm. "Middlings forward!"

The middling dragon riders slipped between the ranks of the grands. They were more like ponies standing beside great horses. Their riders were young men and women of all races, wearing plate-mail armor. Dragon charms emanated around their necks.

"Hold the line!" Justus said.

"Middlings," Commander Shaw said, "attack!"

The middling Riskers rushed forward with fire in their eyes and on their breaths. Their riders drew their bowstrings.

It was exactly what Justus wanted. With the Riskers so close, he could unleash a sneak attack on the enemy. "Now!" he ordered.

The Sky Riders all summoned their wizardry. Within an instant, their minds' invisible fingers ripped the dragon charms away from the necks of their enemies and threw the stones into their very own hands.

The middling dragons reared up and shook their heads as if coming out of a daze.

With the egg-shaped dragon stone resting in the palm of his hand, Justus summoned its power. All together, the Sky Riders turned the middlings against their riders.

The middling dragons attacked with tail, teeth, and claws. Many of them jumped on the backs of the grands.

A horrified look grew quickly on Commander Shaw's, Dirklen's, and Magnolia's faces.

As the dragons and riders attacked one another, Commander Shaw took charge and started barking orders. "Fools! Take to the air! Now!" His grand dragon struck out and bit into the body of a middling. Bones cracked inside the monster's jaws.

The slugfest continued between the Riskers and their dragons. Gradually, they fought their way into the sky.

Once again, the Sky Riders held their ground and let

out a chorus of cheers. High above, the Riskers gathered their forces and regrouped.

"Well done, Yuri, well done." Justus tossed the dragon charm from hand to hand. "Your plan proved quite effective."

"Aye," Hammerjaw agreed.

"Now, with the dragon charms, we can slow down their assault and turn their own power against them," Justus said. "I'd be lying if I said I didn't want to throw Shaw from his saddle."

"If we all focus on the same dragon, that might be possible," Yuri Gnomeknower said as she stood up in her saddle. "The grands are stronger minded than the middlings, but it can be done if we work together."

"That is what we intend to do," he said. "After all, it's worked so far."

Hours passed, and the giants awakened. The rising sun shined over the rim of the crater.

Yuri sat cross-legged beside her dragon, a charm cradled in her palm. Justus just happened to be looking at her when her eyelids snapped open. Her eyes were as big as saucers when she stood.

An icy chill slid down his spine. "What is it, Yuri?"

"Do you remember that dreadful feeling I mentioned before?" she asked.

"Yes," he replied.

"It's back."

17

The thunder of dragon wings grew louder as the Riskers circled below the clouds. They let out triumphant and welcoming roars. The Sky Riders had been resting beside their dragons. Now all of them climbed to their feet, their full attention on the sky.

"Why are they making such a ruckus this time?" Hammerjaw asked as he raked his stubby fingers through his beard. "Do they think that will frighten us?"

Nearby, where the forest met the clearing of the temple's courtyard, Garthar cast a look at Justus. "Black Frost." He ripped a tree out of the ground. "He comes. I can feel him."

"Good, then we can kill him," Hammerjaw said. "That will put end to all of this, won't it?"

Justus's heart raced like a frightened rabbit's. He hadn't

seen Black Frost in over a decade, but now the moment of truth had come. He was going to come face-to-face with his mortal enemy, once and for all. "Is it him?" he asked Firestok.

Firestok gracefully nodded her head. "The giant is right. It could be no one else. But like your heart, mine races as well. I've never felt such... dread."

Black Frost dropped out of the clouds and through the circle of dragons. He dwarfed them all, both middling and grand.

Yuri gasped. She wasn't the only one shocked by the sheer enormity of Black Frost. Stayzie, Mayzie, and Aric joined her disbelief. "It can't be."

"Wh-what is that?" Hammerjaw asked. "Behemoths don't fly the sky. We do."

"That's Black Frost, you fool," Yuri said. "But how?"

Black Frost's pitch-black scales glinted in the sun. He glided through the air with ease, roaring back at the praise of his minions. He was a god among them, towering and fierce. There had never been a creature so large in the sky. He owned it.

"He must be a hundred yards long," Aric commented. "How in Gapoli can that be? Look at him!"

"His girth is great! The middlings are birds among him!" Hogrim said.

Black Frost's talons were sharpened pillars. His scales were the size of blackened iron shields, his head so tremendous that he could possibly swallow a grand dragon whole.

"Yuri, how is this possible?" Justus asked.

"I-I have no idea," she stammered.

"Perhaps it's a trick or an illusion," Mayzie suggested.

Black Frost made several passes over the crater and glided down.

The Gunder pelted him with rocks and trees. Their objects bounced off him like pebbles and sticks. He landed in their midst, crushing the smoldering forest beneath him. He sat on his back legs, towering over the tallest branches.

Garthar marched toward Black Frost and faced him. Even standing tall among the trees, the giant was no more than a child in Black Frost's presence.

Black Frost's deep-blue eyes were like radiant fire. They regarded Garthar with indignation.

"Black Frost, depart from Gunder, or I will destroy you!" Garthar said.

Black Frost responded in a cavernous voice that carried from one end of the crater to the other. "With what, you fool? You cannot hurt me with your stones and fists." He pushed out his chest. "Nothing can."

In his deep, gravelly voice, Garthar replied, "And your fires cannot hurt the Gunder, lizard! Your flames only make us stronger!"

"Is that so?" Black Frost asked. "Perhaps you wish to put me to the test?"

"I've withstood your flames before. I'll withstand them again."

"Ah, then you won't mind me doing this?" Black Frost opened his jaws wide. A waterfall of white fire gushed out of his mouth, consuming Garthar from head to toe.

Garthar pushed his arms and fists outward and above his head. He stood like a mighty tree facing the wind.

Justus's fingernails dug into his palms. He couldn't believe his eyes, and his face beaded with new sweat. The dragon and the giant were far away, but he felt the heat as if he stood right in front of a fireplace.

Black Frost's flames destroyed everything they touched. Garthar's fists shook, and he let out a mighty scream. Slowly, pieces of his body turned to ash. The white flames incinerated his skin and muscle. Somehow, the giant screamed in defiance. The white flames ate away the rest of his body until nothing remained of Garthar except for a giant smoking skeleton standing in a field of incinerated trees.

Black Frost laughed. "Huh, that was easy." His evil gaze sought out the Sky Riders. "Justus. Firestok. You're next."

18

Black Frost's tail lashed out and sent half a dozen warriors spinning head over heels. He blasted them with a cone of white-hot flames.

Justus's heart thumped in his ears. The sheer enormity of Black Frost was shocking enough, but the dragon's firepower was even greater. The Gunder giants, so far as he knew, were impervious to dragon flame, but with a single breath, Black Frost had burned the all-powerful giant's flesh to a crisp.

"How can this be?" Firestok asked, dismayed. "He is impossibly big. No dragon is that big." She turned her head toward Yuri. "Do you know anything of this?"

Yuri squeezed her eyes shut, her face a knot of concentration. "I have no answers. I can only feel him burgeoning with immense power." She opened her eyes. "We must stop him."

"Stop him?" Aric argued. "I'm no coward, but you see what he's doing to the giants. There is a time to fight, and there is a time to flee. Now we must flee."

But Riskers roamed the skies in superior numbers. "There is nowhere to run. The only thing we can do is fight." Justus pulled his sword and took a deep breath. He called out to the Sky Riders. "I don't care how big he is. He must have a weakness. We will find it. Yuri, any suggestions?"

"Let me have the dragon charms. All of them. Perhaps I can slow Black Frost's mind," Yuri said as she opened her hands. The dragon charms that the others held floated from their hands and filled her palms. Using a net of scintillating energy, she caught the charms and clutched them to her belly. "I have no answers as to a weakness, but if I were to guess, I'd say attack him from the inside out."

"What are you suggesting, Yuri?" Hammerjaw asked incredulously. "That we let the dragon swallow us?"

"Something along those lines," she said.

"No one is swallowing this dwarf!" Hammerjaw said.

"And no one can penetrate that breath," Aric said. "You saw what he did to the giants. He'll do the same to us."

Justus spoke up. "Listen, brothers and sisters of the wind. United, we are a weapon that no monster can stand against. We must have faith that our righteous efforts cannot be undone. Together we will summon the wizardry and become one!"

"You aren't suggesting we morph into the Spear of Light?" Aric asked. "It has not been done in centuries, and none of us have even attempted it in our lifetime."

"We've all read, and we've all studied it. Now we have no choice." Justus set his gaze on Black Frost. "It is the only way we can defeat that monster."

"And if we don't?" Aric asked.

"The world will fall," Justus said.

"Let's do this and get it over with. All of this fighting is making me hungry," Hammerjaw said. He rode his dragon over to Justus. "If you want to form the Spear of Light, then I want to be the tip of it."

"So be it! Sky Riders, unite!"

The Sky Riders moved into a diamond formation. Hammerjaw and his dragon took their place in the front. Stayzie and Mayzie doubled up behind Hammerjaw. Justus, Slomander, and Hogrim lined up behind the sisters. Aric and Yuri finished the back of the ranks.

Justus called out to the apprenti. "Take cover inside the temple. You'll be safe there until we return."

"And if we don't return?" Aric asked quietly.

"Then we'll all be sharing a grave." Justus looked back at Yuri. "Are you ready?"

The wizened woman nodded. "I am. Summon the

wizardry. Using the charms, I'll delay Black Frost the best I can. Strike for the heart. It always works."

"Sky Riders," Justus said. "Our time has come. This is what we're made for. Dragons, unite."

The dragons spread their wings until the tips touched. Slowly, they beat their wings and stirred the dust on the ground.

"Sky Riders, call the magic!" Justus sat on Firestok in the center of the group, and he summoned his wizardry. The magic he called started in the pit of his stomach, and his racing heart pumped it through his body. His eyes glowed with fiery intensity, and mystic energy flowed from his fingertips.

The Sky Riders' eyes were aglow, and their bodies radiated with energy. The magic spread between their bodies, connecting them one by one. Energy entered Justus like a crashing wave. The rush of shared power was exhilarating. His mind and his brethren's became one. A field of pure energy formed around them. They shined like a diamond.

In an amplified voice, Justus said, "Fly, Sky Riders! Fly!"

As one, the dragons lifted their Sky Riders from the ground. They jettisoned through the sky and picked up speed as they circled Black Frost from a distance.

With a thought, Justus said, "Yuri, can you feel him?"

"I can," she said. "His mind is as strong as iron. I must concentrate."

Black Frost had burned every living enemy that crossed

his path. He turned his attention to the Sky Riders. "Interesting," he said as he watched them circle by. He followed them with his eyes and twisted his neck to keep them in his sights. "Come, Sky Riders! Attack me with the Spear of Light! Hah! You must have known that I would foresee this! I've forseen everything." He showed his mouthful of razor-sharp teeth. "Including your death!"

19

The Riskers chased the Sky Riders, the dragons attacking with dragon fire while their riders fired arrows. The attacks bounced harmlessly off the Spear of Light's shielding. The Sky Riders gathered speed.

"We have an opportunity to escape, Justus," Aric suggested.

"No, this will be our only chance to kill him." Justus had his attention focused on Black Frost. The evil dragon's eyes stared right back at him and followed their every move.

"What are you waiting for?" Black Frost asked. "You can't use the Spear of Light forever. It will consume you..." His voice trailed off, and he froze.

"Now!" Yuri screamed feverishly. "Now!"

Commanding it with his mind, Justus turned the Spear of Light toward Black Frost. "Strike, Sky Riders! Strike!"

Yuri used the dragon charms to hold Black Frost's mouth wide open. Behind rows of sharp teeth was a gullet the size of a cavern. The Sky Riders would fly right into the soft spots of the dragon's bowels and chew him up.

"Ride the sky!" Hammerjaw hollered. "Ride the sky!"

The Sky Riders soared straight for Black Frost's maw, closing in faster and faster.

Black Frost's frozen stare blinked. His brows knitted together.

"I've lost him!" Yuri said.

"Onward, Sky Riders!" Justus said. There was nothing to stop them from busting Black Frost's teeth out and going in. "Onward!"

Black Frost huffed out a torrent of white-hot fire. The flames slammed into the Spear of Light, enveloping it and slowing its furious trajectory almost to a halt.

"Keep flying, dragons!" Justus hollered.

Inside the protection of the Spear of Light, the Sky Rider dragons' wings beat harder and harder, thrusting them deeper into the fire and toward Black Frost's wide-open maw.

The suffocating heat made it impossible for Justus to catch his breath. His sweat sizzled on his skin. With his eyes squeezed nearly shut, he could barely make out Hammerjaw at the head of the charge. The grizzly dwarf stood on his saddle, with his sword in hand and his arms spread wide. He was hollering something at the top of his lungs.

"Focus on the Spear of Light! Keep it up!" Justus ordered.

The Spear of Light brightened for a moment then quickly began to fade. The mystic coating that covered them all began to crack and fleck away. Up front, the white flames of Black Frost's breath turned Hammerjaw and his dragon to ash. Stayzie's and Mayzie's bodies shriveled into skeletons, and their armor melted like wax.

"Firestok," Justus said as his own body began to peel away. "It's been an honor to serve with you. I'll miss you always and forever." He pictured his niece, Anya, and sent out his final thoughts. "My niece, I hope you are out there. Avenge us."

A deep cold washed over Justus's armor and bones, icing him to the marrow, and suddenly turned to ravenous fire. The last thing he saw was a white flash, and the days of the Sky Riders were over.

COMMANDER SHAW and his troops rounded up all twelve of the Sky Riders' apprenti and had them kneel before Black Frost, with their hands tied behind their backs. Shaw walked behind them.

Six young elven men and six young elven women and not a single one of them trembled.

Black Frost sat with his head held high, his eyes elsewhere.

"By now, all of you have witnessed the awesome force of Black Frost," Shaw said as he slapped his leather glove to his palm. "The giants are dead. Your dragons are dead. And all of the Sky Riders are dead." His glove grazed the back of an elven woman at the end of the row as he passed her. "You can be a part of this. Submit to Black Frost or die."

"I'd rather die," said the elven woman he touched with the glove. Her bright eyes shined, and her jaw muscles clenched.

"You are very spirited. I grant you that," Commander Shaw said. "We could use more of that among our forces. Look at you, all of you. Not one of you quakes with fear. Your bones don't rattle, and your teeth aren't clattering together. I'm surprised. It appears that the Sky Riders prepared you well."

Dirklen stood nearby, facing the apprenti with a sneer on his face. His arms were crossed. "They are well trained. Why don't you let me fight them? After all, I came all this way and didn't get to fight anybody."

Black Frost spit a ball of white flame. It landed on the young elf woman and consumed her. She died instantly, and her crackling body collapsed into ash.

Commander Shaw lifted his brows. "It seems that my

lord Black Frost has lost patience. Who will be the next to serve? Who will be the next to die?"

The elves' faces beaded with new sweat. All of them trembled visibly.

"Time is running out." Commander Shaw squeezed his hand back into his black glove. "Are all of you so foolish that you will give your lives for a cause that is no more?"

None of the apprenti replied.

The wind carried down from the crater's rim, stirring the dead elf's ashes. Ashes from the battle floated through the air like snow.

Commander Shaw shrugged. "So be it." He backed away from the apprenti and looked up at Black Frost. "Your grand worshipfulness, they won't be convinced."

Black Frost's chin dipped as he glowered down at them. "I see." He spit small balls of fire out of his mouth, turning two elves at a time into flames, ash, and smoke.

Only one elf remained, a young male elf, more smallish in build than the others. He shook like a leaf, and his eyes were squeezed closed. He cracked one eye open and looked at the ash piles of his friends. In a shaky voice, he said, "Black Frost, I will serve you!"

"You are very wise for one who appears to be the least of all," Commander Shaw said. "What is your name?"

"Datris." The young elf bowed his head. "What would you have me do?"

"Join the others locating the dragon charms. We need

to see if any of them survived Black Frost's flame." Commander Shaw shooed the youth with his hand. "You are well trained. Go now."

Datris sprinted away and joined the other Riskers searching the grounds. His feet kicked up the dust and ash of the forest.

"Do you have any other orders, Black Frost?" Commander Shaw tilted his head upward. "We are here to do your will."

"What else could we do? He killed all of the Sky Riders," Dirklen said under his breath.

"They aren't all dead," Black Frost said. "I did not see Cinder among them." Using his great paw, he reached down and scooped up the elf named Datris. He lifted the elf before his eyes. "Where are Cinder and his rider?"

Struggling to find the words, Datris said, "They've been gone for days. No one knows where they are. Justus banished Cinder's rider when she helped another apprentice."

Black Frost narrowed his eyes. "Give me names."

"Uh, Anya is the rider, Justus's niece, and Grey Cloak is an elf like me. I never saw much of him."

Black Frost dropped Datris to the ground. He eyed Commander Shaw. "I want them dead, and I want Cinder's head."

Commander Shaw tapped his heels together and saluted. "As you wish, grand worshipfulness."

20

LOOSE BOOT

A loud, roaring yawn woke Anya from her slumber.
Cinder emerged from the frozen layers of a
snowbank that he'd been hidden underneath. He shook
the snow from his head and horns and let out another loud
yawn. It was morning.

"Will you stop that?" Anya was covered in a blanket and
stood by the fire, where the coals grew dim. "You're going to
cause an avalanche."

"Have I been asleep long?" he asked as he wiped snow
from his eyelashes and spread his wings. Piles of snow
dropped to the ground. "You sound bitter."

"Bitter? Me?" She kicked snow over the coals. "Now
why would I be bitter? You've only been asleep over a
month."

"A month isn't very long."

"It is when I've been huddled by a campfire in a frozen wasteland the entire time." She shook out her blanket and folded it up. "Now get out of that snowbank, and let's get going."

Cinder waded out of the bank and shook the snow off like a dog, covering Anya in the white powder. He caught her glare. "Sorry."

"Most days I wish I could fly on my own." She jammed her helmet on and stood in front of him. "Well, warm me up?"

"You could ask nicely."

"You're pushing my temper to the edge, Cinder."

He huffed out steam that melted the snow off her and dried her instantly. "Where is Grey Cloak?"

She climbed into the saddle. "He's been gone for quite some time now."

"The two of you didn't have a falling out, did you?"

"No, but we ran into trouble in Loose Boot. He had to run, and I had to wait!"

"I'm sorry, but I needed to get my sleep. You run me too much, and I am getting older," he said.

Anya sighed. "I don't want to hear your excuses. Let's ride the sky back to Hidemark. I can only imagine that Justus is worried sick."

"As you wish." Cinder pushed off with his powerful legs and launched into the sky. His strong wings beat against the wind and lifted them high above the clouds in seconds.

The warm sun shined on Anya's face, and she basked in its glory. "Finally." She sighed. She'd been waiting for Cinder to wake up for weeks, and she'd had nothing else to do but stew about her decision to save Grey Cloak. She still had her doubts that she did the right thing. Worse, she dreaded facing her brethren of Sky Riders. She had no doubt they would punish her severely.

"How are you doing up there?" Cinder asked.

"I have to admit that I'm feeling better. You?"

"It's good to be flying again. I feel refreshed." He paused. "Anya, I truly am sorry for the delay, but perhaps the time off will serve us for the better. We've been running very hard of late, and I believe it's important to sit back and consider all things."

"Perhaps. But I don't like remaining in one spot for so long. I have to keep moving. Squatting in the snow, day and night, with no one to talk to was torment."

"I understand."

"Do you think the Sky Riders will forgive me?" she asked.

"They are a harsh lot at times. But you know that I'll have to stand trial as well. After all, I let you do it."

"Yes, but you were under my orders."

"There is always a chance that they won't see it that way. Just because I'm a dragon doesn't mean I'm beyond punishment. I can be judged by my own kind too." He shook his head. "I hope Firestok isn't too disappointed in me."

"And I hope Justus isn't too disappointed in me. It wouldn't surprise me one bit if Hammerjaw and some of the others didn't go after him for it."

"As I said, they can be a hard lot." Cinder stretched his wings and glided for leagues. "We aren't in a great hurry, are we? The last time I flew so fast, well, you know what happened. I'd prefer to save my energy."

She closed her eyes and enjoyed the warm sun and wind on her face. "Fly at your own pace. I'm certainly not in a hurry to face my consequences either. But be sure to keep an eye out for the enemy."

"I'll ride the western streams. It's not likely we'll encounter any of them there. In the meantime, pray my vision is keener than theirs, just in case."

"Your vision is the best. I have faith in it."

Cinder flew day and night, and Anya slept off and on. She never felt safer than when she was with Cinder. Flying the skies with him gave her a great sense of security. She dozed off into a deep sleep. Cinder woke her with a gentle buck after what could have been hours or even a day.

"We are approaching Gunder Island," he said with concern.

Anya sat up in the saddle, rubbed her eyes, and yawned. She leaned over and could see they were circling high above the island in the middle of Lake Flugen. It was dusk. "Is something amiss?" she asked.

In a heavy voice, he said, "I spy something horribly wrong."

She squinted. Gunder Island was a dark blip below, and the green trees that filled the crater appeared as dry as a bone. "Fly lower."

Cinder spiraled in a slow descent, gliding on his massive wings, which were stretched wide.

Anya gasped when she got a full look inside Hidemark's crater. The thriving forest had been turned into a wasteland.

21

Anya stepped in ankle-deep ashes that had once made up the trees of Hidemark's forest. She was numb from head to toe as she walked listlessly through the place she called home. It had been turned into a graveyard.

The entire forest, stretching from one end of the crater to the other, over a league of territory, had been burned to the ground. In some places the ground had burned so hot that the earth was as slick as glass. Hardly a tree stood, and the ones that still did were burned to a crisp.

With a fluttering heart, she walked and walked and walked, calling out for her friends and family. "Justus! Aric!"

She had already ventured through the temple in search of answers. The corridors and chambers inside the temple were nothing but ruins. Every table, chair, bed, cot, and storage room had been burned with dragon fire. The armory within had been robbed, and whatever supplies weren't stolen had been destroyed. That would have included suits of dragon armor and weapons the Sky Riders had been building. It was all gone now. And there were no signs of survivors.

Cinder sat in front of the huge skeleton of the Gunder giant Garthar. Somehow, the giant's bones held his massive frame upright on legs as sturdy as tree trunks. Garthar wasn't alone either. He was surrounded by many dead giants whose flesh and muscles had been devoured by fire until only bone was left.

Anya slipped between the dead bodies and, with an incredulous look, said, "I didn't think dragon fire could do this to giants."

"Nor I. It appears we were wrong," Cinder responded in a sad voice. "I've never seen such a force or even imagined it."

"This is the work of Black Frost, isn't it?"

He nodded and looked down. He was sitting inside a dragon's paw print. "He is humongous. Perhaps ten times bigger than me. It's unimaginable."

The handiwork of Black Frost and the Riskers was all around. Dragon prints and footprints covered the ground. They had made no effort to hide their tracks. Whoever had come didn't care about the world knowing they were there.

"We have to keep looking for the others," she said. "Do you think they took them prisoner?"

With a sad look in his eyes, Cinder said, "I don't think they took anyone prisoner. Look around, Anya. Every single Gunder is dead. Black Frost didn't come to take hostages. He came to eliminate the Sky Riders."

She fought back a sob. "Are you saying that all of the Sky Riders are dead? It-it can't be."

Cinder's tail snaked out from behind his body, and with a gentle touch, he brushed the top of a large heap on the ground. The ashes started to crumble and fall away, revealing dragon bones and horns. Every dragon's horns had a unique shape to them.

Anya recognized them immediately. She ran toward the bones. "Firestok!" She dug through the once-beautiful grand dragon's body. "Justus! Justus!" She found an arm detached from its body. Melted metal coated it. "Justus!" Life became a blur as she frantically dug the remains of her family from the ashes.

Cinder did the same.

Together, they uncovered most of the Sky Riders' and dragons' bones, but they found little more than remains. Dragon helms were melted over skulls. Only pieces of bones remained. The ashes were still warm, and the piles of ash reeked of charred skin and burnt hair.

Anya sank to her knees, exhausted, and trembled. She mumbled unintelligibly. "They're gone. They're gone.

They're gone. They're gone. They're all gone." She choked and sobbed in one spot for over an hour. She felt like a hollow shell. "I should have been here. We should have been here."

Cinder crept closer to Anya. He loomed over her and lovingly curled his tail around her body. "Then we would be dead too."

She clutched his tail in her arms, and tears streamed down her face. "Are they really all dead, Cinder? All of them?" She sobbed.

"I'm sorry, but it appears so." Cinder rose, and his tail stiffened. In a hushed voice, he said, "Be still."

Her hand fell to her sword. "Why?"

"Because we are not alone."

22

Anya was on her feet in an instant, and she slid her sword out of her scabbard. She followed Cinder's eyes.

Several dozen yards away, something crept toward them under the ashes. A quick glance around revealed many similar somethings tunneling in their direction, each the size of a crawling man. They formed a half circle around Cinder and Anya and came to a stop a dozen yards away.

Anya narrowed her eyes. She could hear her heart beating inside her ears. Her mind raced. It only made sense that the Riskers would leave some of their legion behind, hoping that more of their enemies would return. She had been careless.

With her sword poised to strike, she crept toward the nearest lump in the ground.

A small dragon—no bigger than a dog—burst out of it and let out an earsplitting shriek. More dragons popped out from underneath the ashes, shrieking like crying babies.

"Fledglings," Cinder said, alarmed. He made a half roar, half growl that silenced the fledglings. "My fledglings. Firestok's fledglings. I know them all." He sank down to the ground and beckoned them over. "Come, children. Come."

The fledglings shook off the ashes and waddled over to him. A dozen of them nestled against his body.

"Know this, Anya. A remnant always survives even the most horrible circumstances. It's a part of life."

"How did they survive?"

"I imagine Firestok sheltered them in Lethas Lagoon. Its enchanted waters protect those near it." He nuzzled his fledglings' cheeks. "They hid, and the enemy overlooked them. We are very blessed."

Anya petted the dragons. "We are, but the rest of our family isn't. They're dead."

"And through us, they live on."

"Cinder, the Sky Riders are wiped out. If I'm the only one left..." Tears streamed down her cheeks. She was dying inside as a pit grew in her belly. She would never see Justus or any of her friends again. Black Frost had killed them. He had killed them all. She gripped her sword tight. "I don't know how, Cinder, but I am going to kill that dragon. I don't care how big he is. He is going to die."

"And I support you wholeheartedly. We will find a way, Anya," he said. "We will."

THEY SPENT the rest of the night and the better part of the following morning making graves for their fallen friends. Anya took any salvageable remains of the Sky Riders, such as pieces of their armor and helmets, and made burial spots inside the temple's chambers.

Outside, Cinder dug up the earth and buried what he could of the dragons in the dirt. In some cases, the dragon scales had survived and hung loose over their bones, but Black Frost's flames had ravaged all of the muscle and marrow. Cinder held Firestok's skin in his claws like a rag.

"What are you going to do with that?" Anya asked.

"I know that it is sacrilege, but the scales survived. I'm curious. It appears that Black Frost's flame can't destroy everything," he said.

"No, but it cooked the dragons from the inside out." Her stomach rolled just thinking about it. "You aren't really going to carry Firestok's skin, are you? It's morbid."

"I suppose that you're right. I'll bury it."

"Good idea. In the meantime, what are we going to do with the fledglings? Take them with us? I have no doubt that Black Frost will be looking for us."

"We have to start over again, Anya."

"Start over with what?" she asked. "In case you haven't noticed, I'm the last Sky Rider."

He nodded. "Yes, you are the last that we know of, meaning you are in charge."

She tilted her head to one side. "I'm in charge of what? You? Fledglings? You know that I can't do this by myself." She adjusted the buckles on her bracers. "I'm too young, and I've never been in charge before." She blew a strand of wavy red hair from her eyes. "And where are we going to train and rebuild? If we can't hide here and survive with the protection of the giants, where will we go?"

"There is always the Wizard Watch. Perhaps they will have answers." He watched a trio of fledglings crawl over his spine. "And you aren't alone."

"I know. I have you and them, I guess."

"I'm not talking about us."

"Then who?"

"What about Grey Cloak? He's a Sky Rider, isn't he?"

"He was a Sky Rider, but he's banished," she said.

"Look around, Anya. He's banished from what? And you're in charge now."

She propped her foot on a stone and tightened the laces on her boots. "Huh. So I'm the commander of the Sky Riders, and I can make any decision I want. That almost sounds like a dream come true, aside from the fact that I'm the only benefactor of my brethren's deaths. That's not right. Is it, Cinder?"

He shrugged his wings. "Who is to say that it's wrong? Me?"

"Hmph, I suppose not, but I hardly think Grey Cloak is reliable. He had no desire to become a Sky Rider. He was always more concerned about his freedom." An uncontrollable grin crossed her face, and she quickly stifled it before Cinder saw. She liked the idea of having Grey Cloak around. In their brief time together, she'd become very fond of him, more than she would like to admit. And she couldn't help but find it funny that he would choose a runt dragon out of the litter over all the others. "There's no telling where in the world he might be, and it's not like we can fly you right into the heart of every city."

"You're making excuses."

"No, I'm being practical."

"I see. Well, one way or the other, *you* need to warn the world about Black Frost and what he did and pray that they listen."

She scooped up a fledgling in her arms. "And why wouldn't they?"

"People don't like bad news, Anya. They cover their ears and hope it goes away. By the time they listen, quite often, it is too late."

She gathered up more dragons and put them on Cinder's back. "I suppose we're off to see the nearest Wizard Watch, then."

"It sounds like as good a place to start as any."

23

MONARCH CITY

Grey Cloak squatted on a ledge overlooking a cavernous dungeon. Fifty feet below him was the floor of a huge cavern that had been turned into a network of dungeons and cells where slaves were kept. He could see the prisoners' hands reaching through the bars as they begged for food from the guards who passed. Their moaning and misery echoed throughout the dungeon.

The guards were lizardmen, brawny in build, with thick tails dragging behind their bodies. They whipped their leather lashes at the fingers that stretched toward them. The prisoners groaned, their pleas desperate and, in some cases, deranged.

Dyphestive kneeled down behind Grey Cloak and bumped him hard.

Grey Cloak rocked forward and caught himself before he fell over the edge.

"Sorry," Dyphestive whispered.

"Will you be more careful? The whole point of sneaking into a dungeon is to not get caught," Grey Cloak looked his blood brother up and down. Dyphestive's still-growing, hulkish form shielded Grey Cloak like a boulder. The expression on his brother's face was amiable, as always. "I think dragging an anchor would be easier than hauling you around."

"Anchors don't have legs."

"And they don't talk either. Now, will you be quiet? We have a princess to save."

"She's a princess?"

"She is to her parents. That's all that matters." He opened up his cloak, and Streak slipped out from underneath it.

The runt dragon had grown to be about thirty pounds of ruddy scales and muscle. His head was as flat and broad as a shovel, and two black stripes raced down the spiny ridges of his back. His pink tongue flickered out of his mouth. His citrine eyes showed a haunting intelligence as he peered over the ledge.

Crunch. Crunch. Crunch.

Grey Cloak's head sank into his shoulders. Slowly he twisted his head around. Dyphestive was eating an apple. "What, pray tell, are you doing?"

"I'm eating."

Grey Cloak didn't hide his disdain. "Why?"

Dyphestive stopped chewing. "Because I'm hungry."

"Swallow it."

"What?"

"I said swallow it. I can't have you making any more noise or leaving a trail of apple cores for our enemies to follow."

"Don't worry about that. I always eat the whole thing. Besides, the seeds are good for you. Crane says so—*ulp*."

Grey Cloak shoved the apple into his brother's mouth and covered Dyphestive's mouth with his hand.

Wide-eyed, Dyphestive swallowed the remains whole.

Grey Cloak removed his hand. "No more food. Now be quiet." He turned his attention back to the dungeons below. His gray eyes narrowed, and his gaze moved from the cells to the several cages that hung above the dungeon floor, suspended by chains. Some held bodies, and some didn't.

It had been over a year since they came to Monarch City and Rhonna, Lythlenion, and Tanlin departed. He, Dyphestive, Zora, and Crane remained. They still referred to themselves as Talon but discretely. It took them a couple of weeks to settle in, but Grey Cloak quickly fell in love with the huge city. It had a little bit of everything: great food, entertainment, and droves of people from all over the world. Every day he saw something that he hadn't seen before, and it enthralled him.

With Crane driving the carriage, the remaining trio quietly started making a name for themselves by serving people in need, wealthy people Crane had connections with who paid well. Talon was on a mission now to save a young girl and boy who were snatched by slavers that worked in the dark underbelly of Monarch City. The children were being held for ransom.

"How are we going to know what they look like?" Dyphestive asked, his lips almost touching the tip of Grey Cloak's ear.

Grey Cloak pushed his brother's face back. "They already told me. Youths. Brown hair and blue eyes. They'll respond to their names."

Dyphestive looked over Grey Cloak's shoulder. "There are a lot of guards and cages down there. How are we going to find them?"

"Will you be silent and stop asking the obvious?"

"If I'm silent, I won't be asking anything."

"That's the point. And if you'd listen more and eat less, you would already know the answer to your question. Zora is down there now."

Dyphestive craned his neck. "Really? I don't see her."

"That's because she's invisible. Remember the Scarf of Shadows that Tanlin gave her?"

Dyphestive nodded.

"She'll find them. Once she finds them, we'll have to figure out a way to free them."

"What about the others?"

"We can't free them all. We can only free the ones we are paid to free."

Dyphestive's eyebrows buckled.

"Brother, we aren't freeing all of them. We don't even know who all of them are. Maybe they're supposed to be imprisoned."

"That doesn't seem right." Dyphestive rubbed his square jaw. "So long as we're here, we might as well free them all."

"We have to free the ones we came for first."

"So, we will free them all."

"No, I didn't say that. What I'm saying is that we need to free the Gunthys' children. They are being held for ransom. We don't know about the others. First things first." He stroked Streak's back as he spoke. "And we'll alert the authorities about the rest since we found them too."

"Why don't we tell the Honor Guard we found them in the first place?"

"Because then we wouldn't get paid. And the Gunthys want to keep this quiet for their own reasons." Grey Cloak shook his head and ran his fingers down his face. "Next time, you're staying home."

24

"**W**hy don't the Gunthys pay the ransom?" Dyphestive asked. "Wouldn't that be easier?"

"Perhaps they don't have the money. Perhaps they don't want to. I don't know. We don't ask those questions," Grey Cloak said. They'd been bickering back and forth for minutes. Dyphestive had one question after the other. For years, Dyphestive had never questioned anything that Grey Cloak said, but now he was questioning their intentions behind everything. "Again, you don't have to come if you don't want to. Zora and I can handle it on our own."

Streak's throat rattled.

"Pardon me. Zora, Streak, and I can handle this on our own."

"But then I wouldn't get paid."

"Since when do you care about money?"

Dyphestive grinned. "Since I started eating more."

"Enough. Here she comes."

"I don't see her."

"No, but I can hear her." Grey Cloak's keen hearing picked out Zora's soft footsteps as they came up a narrow staircase carved in the stone leading up to their position. He scooted back into Dyphestive and tried to push him back. It was like trying to move a wall. "Will you make some room?"

They huddled on the ledge, away from any prying eyes below.

Zora reappeared and pulled the Scarf of Shadows down from her nose. Her warm green eyes sparkled in the dimness. Her auburn hair was shoulder-length, and she was as pretty as ever. "Goy, it stinks down there. Next time, you can use the scarf and take a peek yourself."

Grey Cloak reached for her scarf. "I'd be glad to."

She slapped his hand away. "Keep dreaming."

"You know you're always in my dreams," he said.

Zora rolled her eyes. "Not this again." She wiped the sweat from her brow onto her sleeve. "Anyway, back to business. I found them." She got a sad look in her eye.

"They aren't dead, are they?"

"No, but they are pitiful and frightened. I don't think they've been fed, or at least, they haven't eaten. Their clothing is filthy, and the dirt on their faces is streaked with tears."

Dyphestive's jaws clenched. "That's awful."

"Did you speak with them?" Grey Cloak asked.

"No. My gut told me that if I did, they'd let the entire dungeon know. I couldn't risk it." She eyed their surroundings and took a quick peek over the rim. "Getting them out of there is going to be a very delicate operation. The Dark Addler's minions are hard at work."

Grey Cloak tapped his fingers together and contemplated their situation with the Dark Addler.

The Dark Addler was a brotherhood of thieves, smugglers, slavers, and kidnappers that everyone knew about but no one talked about. Crane had warned them about the Dark Addler when they arrived at Monarch City. He'd said, "Don't make waves" with them. According to Crane, the Dark Addler was run by the Monarchs, a secret society designed to keep the citizens living in fear while the Monarchs offered their protection. Supposedly, if any one family crossed the Monarchs, they would use the Dark Addler as their enforcers. But those were only rumors. No one could prove it, Crane said, and if they could, it wasn't likely that they would live to tell about it.

"Can we be certain that this is the work of the Dark Addler?" he asked Zora.

"It's a large operation. Not to mention that this dungeon is right below one of the Monarchs' cathedrals," she said. "You're worried about what Crane said, aren't you?"

"He did tell us to avoid them."

Dyphestive put a heavy hand on Grey Cloak's shoulder and squeezed. "We aren't going to leave those children."

"Of course not. I'm only clarifying what we're dealing with. And so far, all I see is a bunch of lizardmen guarding a bushel of prisoners. The trick is getting the ones we want out of there. Where are they, exactly, by the way?"

Zora pointed down at the cages hanging from the ceiling. "The caverns tunnel around the bend, and there are more cells and cages hanging above. They're in the last one."

"Are there more guards down there?" he asked.

"Not lizardmen."

"What do you mean by *not lizardmen*?"

"It's an ogre," she said with a worried look.

"Fine, it's an ogre. We can handle an ogre. After all, they are very dumb. A simple distraction of sorts should do it."

"He's a big one with four arms," she added. "He stands so tall that he can reach up into the cages. His head bumps them when he walks. I saw it."

"Well, you know the saying: 'the bigger the ogre, the dumber they are.'"

Zora crinkled her nose. "And smellier. I swear I can taste the stink."

"All right, well here is the plan. I count six guards. We'll lure them into a vacant cell, and you'll use the Ring of Mist to knock them out. That'll leave the ogre." He made a curious expression. "What does one call a four-armed ogre?"

"A fogre," Zora said matter-of-factly.

"Then why didn't you call him that in the first place? Hah hah." He put his index fingers up. "We'll take the guards out first, then we'll deal with this *fogre*." He turned to face Dyphestive. "You stay here and guard our exit. This is the back entrance, and that is the front entrance." He jabbed his finger at a set of stairs that led up to an iron gate securing the dungeon area. "I assume that leads back to the cathedral, but I don't know. Maybe it goes to the Monarchs' castle. It took me long enough to find this secret entrance." He nodded to Zora. "Are you ready?"

25

While all of the prisoners were secured in their cells, the lizardmen guards sat at a table, playing a game of cards called birds. They ate gruel from clay bowls with wooden spoons and drinking flagons of mead. The lizardmen were strong fighters, good soldiers, but they weren't the smartest. They had a lazy way of doing things and relied more on a force of numbers than brains.

From the shadows, Grey Cloak, Zora, and Streak watched the guards' every move.

"They appear to be settled in. I think it's time for you to make your entrance," Grey Cloak said to her. "Be careful."

"Don't worry. I won't let them lay a hand on me." With a playful smile, she strutted over to the table where the brutes huddled over their cards, shielding them with their broad, muscular backs. She tapped the dealer on the shoulder. "Do you have room for one more?"

The lizardmen looked up. The narrow slits of their serpentine eyes widened. Their cards fell out of their hands. They jumped up from the table, and their fingers fumbled for their clubs and lashes.

"Who are you?" the dealer demanded, clearly the leader of the others, who kept silent. He smoked a pipe and held a black wooden rod in his hand.

She addressed them all. "I'm one of the new guards. They're bringing on a new half-elf division." She saluted. "I'm here to guard the prisoners and take all of your chips while we play the birds." She giggled. "Sorry, fellas, only trying to break the tension. All of you look so surprised. Didn't you get the notification? Commander Slurpslop sent it over this morning."

The lizardmen exchanged dumb looks with one another. All except one. The dealer. He glared down at her and, with a hint of intelligence, said, "There is no Commander Slurpslop." He poked her in the chest and knocked her a full step backward. "I don't know who you are." He poked her again, pushing her back. "Or how you came down here, but you're coming with me."

Zora rose up on her tiptoes, poked the lizardman in the chest, and said, "Goy! You listen to me. I'm a new recruit, and more of us are coming. So whether you know Commander Slurpslop or not isn't my problem." She kept poking him in the chest. He backed up. "You're the problem!"

Grey Cloak's fingernails dug into his palms. He was used to seeing Zora act, but this time she was really laying it on thick. *She's crazy.*

"STOP POKING ME, woman, or I will toss you in a cell and lock you up!" the lizardman leader said. He stood his ground. "Now, you will stay still until we sort this out."

Zora chuckled and snatched the black club from his grip, twirling it over her palms. "I can only assume that my men will be issued one of these. They are very heavy. Do you have any that are lighter?"

"Give me that!" The lizardman reached for the club.

She tossed the club high in the air, sending the club spinning end over end. The lizardmen looked up. She kept her eyes down and unleashed a hard kick to the leader's groin.

The leader dropped to a knee. The club fell and bounced off the top of his head. He blinked several times and made an angry snarl. "Get her!"

The other five lizardmen pounced at her as one. Zora skipped away like a deer springing through a meadow. She dashed by the cauldrons of fire and raced by the prisoners' cells. The prisoners pushed their desperate faces to the bars and cheered her on. The lizardmen came at her as one unit. They grabbed at her feet, crashed into the floor, and tripped over one another.

Zora picked up a water bucket and slung it into a lizardman's face. The bucket crashed against the side of his head, and liquid burst everywhere. She jumped over a lizardman's tail as it lashed out at her. All the while, she spoke.

"Commander Slurpslop is going to be very upset when he discovers how you treated me." She kicked another lizardman in the groin. "Is this some sort of initiation? This is fun." She leg-swept two lizardmen, one right after the other. "For me, anyway." She backpedaled from two more attackers. "I have to tell you, for guards, you aren't very good at this."

The winded lizardmen's chests heaved, and they foamed at the mouth. Zora had run circles around them.

"And you appear to be very out of shape. It's no wonder you're so good as guards and nothing else."

The leader snuck up behind her. He lunged and tried to wrap his arms around her. She ducked underneath them and crawled between his legs. She bounced up and kicked him in the back, propelling him forward into the rest of his men.

The lizardmen started to chase her, but their leader said, "Stop! We look like fools!"

"That's because you are fools." Zora backed toward an open cell on the end.

The leader wagged his club at her. "Spread out, men!" He took a deep breath. His broad chest expanded. "I don't know who you are, but you won't be leaving this dungeon on my watch."

The lizardmen advanced.

Zora backed into the dead end where the last cell stood open.

"Hah! We have you now."

"You fools don't have me at all," she said. "Look at you, so dumb you can't even lace your boots."

Five of the six lizardmen looked down but not the leader. She laughed.

"Idiots! Your boots are tied!" the leader said. "Get her!"

Zora raced into the cell. It was at least ten feet deep and almost as wide. She stood with her back against the wall and watched as the lizardmen crowded in.

The leader placed his fists on his hips and let out a raspy laugh. "Hah, you have nowhere to run now, little rabbit."

26

Zora managed a smile. "I'm warning you. You're making an enormous mistake. After all, you are assaulting a high-ranking member of the Dark Addler."

The lizardmen exchanged uncertain looks.

"She's bluffing," the leader said. "The Dark Addler doesn't play games like this." He smacked his club into his hand. "But I will show you what the Dark Addler does when you mess with their servants."

"Well, you've done a fascinating job so far." She lifted her scarf over her nose and vanished.

The lizardmen looked like they'd swallowed bugs.

"What happened? Where did she go?" the leader asked.

Without hesitation, Zora crawled on hands and knees right between their legs and out of the cell. There, Grey

Cloak and Streak were waiting. As soon as she was out, Grey Cloak slammed the cell door shut.

The lizardmen twisted around and charged. They rammed into the door just as Grey Cloak secured a padlock on the cell. They beat on the bars.

"Let us out of here!" the leader said.

Zora dropped the scarf from her nose and revealed herself.

The lizardmen gasped, and their eyes widened.

"That took you long enough, and there was an awful lot of jibber jabber," Grey Cloak said.

"What's the matter? Did I use even more showmanship than you would have?" she replied.

The lizardmen were going wild and jerking on the bars.

"We'll kill you!" the leader shouted.

Grey Cloak and Zora continued as casually as if they were in a tavern café, drinking coffee. "In my case, it wasn't flashy enough, but in your case, I think you were pushing it." He rolled his hand. "Let's get on with it before they start making more of a racket."

"Why the hurry? Don't you enjoy the gentle musings of lizardmen?" On her right hand, she wore a ring fashioned like a small dark sunflower. She held it before the lizardmen's faces while speaking to Grey Cloak. "I hope they like lullabies."

Grey Cloak backed away and covered his nose.

A fine white mist spewed from Zora's ring. The mist

spread over the lizardmen's snouts. They began coughing and choking. Their legs buckled, and they dropped to the floor, fast asleep.

After the mist cleared, Grey Cloak stepped up to the bars. "You haven't ever used that ring on me, have you?"

Zora pursed her lips, blew on the top of her ring, and winked. "You wouldn't remember if I did."

"You're something else, Zora."

"That, I know."

"Come on, then. Let's see what we have to do to take this fogre out." The prisoners in the cells stretched their arms between the bars as he passed. They begged him to free them. They were hapless, disheveled, tired eyed, and grimy. He looked away.

"Should we do something?" Zora asked.

"First things first." He stopped at the last cell in front of the row that bent around the corner. "You said this four-armed ogre is guarding the cells in this next row?"

She nodded. "He's a big one and sits right underneath the Gunthys' cage."

"I see." He peeked around the corner. Sure enough, a beastly ogre sat underneath a cage at the end of the dungeon row. He was a mountain of slab, sweat, coarse hair, and muscle. "Zooks, his neck is thicker than your waist."

"My waist?"

"Well, barely."

She punched his arm.

"What? I said barely."

"What are we going to do? Kill the fogre?" she asked.

"I don't see much of a recourse if we can't trap him in one of those cells. We all know that knocking an ogre out is nearly impossible. Hmmm..." He rubbed his chin and glanced at the iron portcullis at the main entrance. "I have an idea. We'll lure him to the other side of the iron gate, then we'll slip out the back door."

Dyphestive crept up behind them. "Greetings."

Grey Cloak almost broke his neck turning around. "What are you doing here? You were supposed to be guarding the back door."

"I closed it."

"You donkey skull. Who is going to warn us if someone comes?"

"I locked it."

Grey Cloak's frown deepened. "That's not what you were supposed to do. You were supposed to watch our backs."

"But won't it be easier to go out that way?" Dyphestive asked.

"No, because that's the main exit, which will most likely lead us back to the enemy that kidnapped the striplings in the first place."

Dyphestive scratched his head. "Oh."

Grey Cloak tried to sound patient. "Now, will you please go back to your post and let us handle this?"

"If you say so." Dyphestive patted Zora on her shoulder. "That was an impressive feat you achieved. Good job."

"Thank you," she replied pleasantly.

As Dyphestive turned and headed back toward his post, a loud pounding started on the other side of the back door. He turned toward Grey Cloak. "I think someone is coming."

Grey Cloak clapped a hand to his forehead.

27

The ogre rose from his seat and almost bumped his head on the Gunthy children's cage. He was a massive eight-footer with gummy eyes and rotting teeth. Most of his stringy hair had fallen out of the top of his head. He wandered forward, his four long arms hanging at his sides. His melon-shaped head rocked from shoulder to shoulder.

"Great, look who's coming over to investigate," Grey Cloak said.

Holding the war mace Thunderash in his hands, Dyphestive said, "I can handle him."

"Hold your horseshoes, and wait a moment. Let him pass, and if he doesn't see us, we'll slip by"—Grey Cloak made a sweeping gesture with his hands—"and free the striplings."

"Why don't we free all of them?" Dyphestive suggested.

"Gunthys first. Rabble later. Do you understand?"

The pounding at the upper-level back door grew louder, the hard hammering echoing throughout the great chamber. The men and women in the cells and cages screamed, "Free me! Free me! Free me!"

"I think you should free the prisoners first." The new voice came from inside the cell they stood beside. Its prisoner had remained huddled in the back, and now he came forward. His piercing eyes were golden brown, and his long gray hair had rusty streaks.

"Horseshoes, Grey! It's that hermit from Farhook!" Dyphestive exclaimed.

"Will you keep your voice down? I can see that," Grey Cloak replied with growing disappointment. He took a quick look and watched the fogre wander right by them toward the back-entrance steps. "What are you doing here, hermit?"

"Following you," the hermit replied in a scratchy voice.

"What do you mean you're following me? You can't be following me, because I only arrived here moments ago." He shook his head. "Oh, never mind."

"Say, let me out. You have the keys?" The hermit stretched his scaly hands through the bars. "Gimme, gimme."

"Ignore him." He shoved Zora in the back. "Let's go lower that cage."

The three of them ran underneath the suspended cages, making a beeline for the one in the back. The prison cells on that side of the dungeon were dark inside and silent. When they reached the last cage, the children inside were already standing. Their small hands clutched the metal bars, and the half-orc striplings trembled like leaves.

Grey Cloak put a finger to his lips. "Keep quiet, Gunthys. Your parents sent us to bring you home." He nodded at the wall where chains kept the cages suspended using a crank and lever. "Can you handle that?" he asked Dyphestive.

Dyphestive headed to the crank on the wall, pulled the release lever, and started lowering the cage.

"Go see what the ogre's status is," he said to Zora. The bend in the dungeon cells concealed them from the fogre's eyes but also kept him hidden from them.

She ran to the end of the aisle and hollered back. "He's climbing the stairs."

"Great," he said. "Hurry up, Festive!"

The muscles in Dyphestive's naked arms bulged and flexed as the chain links rattled. The cage looked like a ton of steel. It lowered to the ground and made an audible rattling boom.

Grey Cloak went to work picking the padlock on the door. "Horseshoes, this thing is so old, the mechanism has rusted."

"Let me help," Dyphestive said.

Grey Cloak stepped aside.

Dyphestive bashed the padlock with Thunderash.

The orcen striplings kicked the door open with their filthy bare feet. They rushed into Dyphestive's arms. They squeezed his neck as hard as they could. "Take us home! Take us home!"

"Grey Cloak, we're going to have company!"

The blood brothers arrived alongside Zora just as the fogre opened the back entrance. Lizardmen soldiers came pouring from the opening.

"Well, that's going to be a problem," Grey Cloak said.

"Listen to me, elf." The hermit spoke again. "If you let us prisoners out, we might be able to help."

"If I let you out, they might kill you too. Sorry, but you are safer in your cells than out."

"You're making a mistake. You'll regret it," the hermit warned.

Grey Cloak tuned out the hermit. The only thing that mattered was getting the striplings to safety. He pointed at the main entrance's iron portcullis. "That way!"

With the orc striplings in one arm and the battle mace in the other, Dyphestive followed Grey Cloak and Zora up the steps. "I don't feel right about this."

"We can't leave the striplings in harm's way either," Grey Cloak replied. "Sorry, but we've simply run out of time."

On the top ledge, the lizardmen shouted, "Halt!" at the

top of their lungs while the four-armed ogre bounded down the steps.

The heroic trio crossed over the iron gate's threshold just as Grey Cloak pulled the lever to lower it. The gate rattled downward. He motioned toward the wide stone staircase leading up. "There's our exit."

At the top of the steps was a large set of wooden double doors overlaid with black iron. The doors burst open, and at least a score of lizardmen, armed to the teeth with spears, poured out.

"Dyphestive, grab the portcullis!" Grey Cloak ordered.

Dyphestive set the striplings down just in time to grab the gate before it closed. "Hurry! This thing is heavy!"

Grey Cloak, Zora, and the children rolled underneath the gate. Grey Cloak grabbed the lever and pushed it back up.

"Grey, look out!" Zora yelled.

The fogre climbed the steps and chased Grey Cloak away from the lever. He shoved it back down with two of his arms and roared at Grey Cloak.

The gate lowered, trapping Dyphestive on the other side, leaving him outnumbered twenty to one.

28

Life-and-death decisions took split seconds to make. Grey Cloak's mind raced as he considered all the possibilities. The lizardmen that had rushed in from the back entrance were coming down the stairs. The four-armed ogre guarded the lever to raise the iron portcullis. Dyphestive was a sitting duck, trapped on the other side of the gate, and a score of lizardmen were coming down the entrance steps, with spears poised to kill.

Grey Cloak's fingers fished in the pockets of the Cloak of Legends, which he proudly wore. He produced two slender, corked vials. He passed one through the bars to Dyphestive. "Drink this now!"

Dyphestive eyed his enemies, with his war mace gripped in his hands. "But I'm not thirsty."

"Take it now, or you're going to become a shish kebab!"

Grey Cloak stuffed the vial into Dyphestive's meaty grip. At the same time, the second wave of lizardmen charged across the dungeon floor, making a beeline for him and Zora. "Zora, get away from those steps."

Zora sprang backward from the middle of the staircase to the top of the landing.

Grey Cloak tossed the second vial, smashing it on the bottom steps. A sparkling-blue liquid burst on the stone stairs and spread rapidly, covering the entire staircase in ice.

The first three lizardmen raced up the stairs, slipped, and tumbled downward, one on top of the other.

"Look out!" Zora shouted.

Grey Cloak ducked just in time to avoid the ogre's great arms trying to clutch him from behind. He drew his sword and stabbed one of the ogre's four hands.

The ogre's painful roar would have woken the dead.

Grey Cloak cringed. "Zooks, that was loud. Zora, I'll distract him. You push that lever back up."

The ogre wasn't a fool. He guarded the lever with his life. "No, no, no! No one leaves this dungeon of mine."

Zora flicked a dagger and hit the ogre in the middle of the forehead. The dagger stuck in his skull right between his eyes.

The ogre pulled the dagger out. He slammed it on the ground and sent it bouncing. "Don't like that!"

"I hit him in the head, and he doesn't even blink. You

stab his hand, and he screams like a baby." She readied another dagger. "I guess it's true that ogres' skulls are harder than rocks."

The lizardmen continued to slip and slide at the bottom of the stairs while Grey Cloak came up with another idea. He pulled a dagger from his belt and summoned his wizardry, charging the weapon with blue light. "Eat my thunderbolt!" He flung it at the ogre.

The dagger sailed straight and true in a streak of light. It slipped between the ogre's massive arms and exploded in the ogre's broad chest.

The ogre let out a painful growl and stumbled back into the wall behind him. His pumpkin head smacked against a stone ledge and broke it.

Grey Cloak jumped twenty feet in a single spring and pushed up the lever to the iron gate.

DYPHESTIVE TORE the cork off the slender vial with his teeth and guzzled the contents down. The lumpy liquid burned on its way down his throat. "Blecht." He smacked his lips and spit the foul taste from his mouth. "That was awful."

The lizardmen created a half-circle wall of spears two rows deep before him. They narrowed their yellow eyes and thrust their spear tips toward him.

Dyphestive twirled his war mace in his hands. He had

trained with the Doom Riders, the greatest fighters in the world. He could handle a score of lizardmen, probably. "I'll be happy to accept your surrender. If not, this is going to get real ugly."

The leader of the lizardmen stepped forward. He wore an open-faced helmet that fit oddly on his reptilian head. The shoulder pads of his armor had golden tassels. He spoke with a hiss, as most lizardmen did. "You surrender, or you will become my soldiers' pin cushion." His eyes suddenly widened.

Dyphestive's skin started to itch. His bare arms broke out in hard lumps. "Bloody horseshoes, what is happening?" The bumps rose all over is body, turning his skin into an armor of smooth river-stone-shaped rocks. He gawped as he looked at his stony gray hand.

The leader of the lizardmen raised his arm. "First wave, kill him!"

The lizardmen launched their spears at Dyphestive.

He couldn't help but jump away. The spears bounced off his body, the long shafts clattering to the floor.

Dyphestive dropped his arms from his face. He didn't have a scratch on him. He looked at the lizardmen and grinned, exposing a mouthful of gray teeth. "This is going to be fun." He cocked Thunderash underneath his shoulder and charged.

"Second wave, attack!" the leader ordered.

The lizardmen thrust their spears into Dyphestive's

charge. Spear shafts snapped, and the tips chipped against his body.

He unleashed a wide-arcing swing and busted into two lizardmen at once, knocking them into three more. He brought Thunderash down on their skulls and knocked their sharp teeth out. With his war mace, he clubbed them, and with his free hand, he punched their faces.

The lizardmen scrambled away from Dyphestive's powerful onslaught. They abandoned their weapons and tackled him onto the stairs.

He headbutted, bit, kicked, and elbowed. With an inhuman growl, he tore away from their strong limbs and brought the war mace down again. Broken bodies quickly piled up at his feet.

Lizardmen limped up the stairs away from him. The leader shouted commands at his men. "Stand your ground! Pin his arms and legs, you fools! He is only one. We are many!"

Dyphestive threw a haymaker and knocked several teeth out of a lizardman's mouth. His knee caught another underneath the chin and snapped its head backward. A lizardman locked his arms around Dyphestive's ankle and bit it. His teeth broke on Dyphestive's stony skin. With his blue eyes ablaze, Dyphestive hammered away at every desperate lizardman that came at him. He felled them in ones, twos, and threes. But the lizardmen were as tough as their thick skins, and they fought on. Over half of them were dead or knocked out cold.

Sharp pain drew Dyphestive's attention to his thigh, where a lizardman had sunk its teeth into his skin. He dropped his war mace. The potion had worn off. He bled. "Horseshoes."

Under the command of their leader, the lizardmen gathered their spears and regrouped. Their leader pointed at Dyphestive's wounds. "He bleeds. He dies. Kill him!"

29

"Dyphestive, quit playing with those lizardmen, and get over here!" Grey Cloak shouted. He held the lever to the iron drop gate, but the ogre was coming.

"Coming!" Dyphestive dropped to the ground and rolled underneath the iron gate.

Grey Cloak pulled the lever down, and the gate started to drop again.

"Thunderash!" Dyphestive stretched his long arm beneath the closing gate and grabbed the war mace's handle. The lizardmen stabbed at his arm and hand. He jerked the mace to the other side.

The drop gate slammed down, and the lizardmen crashed into it.

"Grey Cloak, we need to get out of here. The ice is melting!" Zora shouted.

The lizardmen on the inside of the gate were starting to make the climb up the ice-covered steps.

The ogre rushed Grey Cloak, and he sprang away.

"My lever!" the ogre said as he pushed it up.

The drop gate started to lift. The lizardmen on the other side crouched low and crawled underneath it.

Dyphestive charged the ogre and slammed his war mace into the monster's shoulder. The ogre let out a howl and released the lever, giving Dyphestive the opportunity to shove the lever back into place. The drop gate fell, pinning several screaming lizardmen underneath.

The ogre snarled, and Dyphestive snarled back. They charged each other like rams. Dyphestive unleashed a well-timed swing to the skull. The surprisingly agile ogre grabbed the mace by the handle with both of his right hands. He started pummeling Dyphestive in the face with his left. Over five hundred pounds of ogre muscle beat on Dyphestive like a drum. He absorbed one blow after another to the face.

"Let go of your mace, you fool, and hit him back!" Grey Cloak shouted. He'd seen Dyphestive take his share of beatings before, but this was out of hand. He thrust his sword into the ogre's leg.

The ogre took a backhanded swipe at him.

He ducked and rolled away.

"Grey Cloak!" Zora screamed.

Two lizardmen had cornered her against the wall at the top of the steps.

"You're on your own, brother!" He sprang across the landing and stabbed one of the lizardmen in the back.

Zora pinned two of her daggers in the other lizardman's chest. Two were dead, but more were coming, at least another score of them.

Out of the corner of his eye, Grey Cloak caught the two children cowering in the corner. The brother covered the sister with his body. "Streak!" Grey Cloak pointed to the striplings. "Protect them! Zora, we're going to need some help."

She kicked a lizardman back down the icy steps. "What do you want me to do?"

"Start freeing the prisoners from their cells."

"Oh, now you want to free us!" the hermit shouted over the commotion of battle.

"Let him out last," Grey Cloak said of the hermit. "Can you handle it?"

Zora winked. "You know I can." She lifted her scarf over her nose and vanished.

He turned his attention back to Dyphestive. The ogre had his brother in a four-armed bear hug, and they were exchanging headbutts.

Grey Cloak ran back across the landing at the top of the stairs, cutting down two lizardmen as he passed. "Now what are you doing?" he asked his brother.

"I'm using my head!" Dyphestive headbutted the ogre again. Their skulls cracked loudly.

Grey Cloak winced. "We don't have time for this! Stop fooling with the ogre now!" He gored a lizardman that rushed him just as he finished his sentence. "Time is running out!"

"I only need a little longer." Dyphestive took another shot to his head. His face was red and swollen like a tomato. "I'm winning!"

Back and forth, Dyphestive and the ogre went at it like two rams smashing horns.

"Have it your way." Grey Cloak turned and faced a new pair of lizardmen with studded clubs who topped the stairs and charged. He stood as still as a crane and watched them come. By his standards, they moved as if stuck in molasses. He knew what they were going to do before they even swung. With only five steps separating him from them, he lunged in between them and buried his sword and dagger into their hearts. The lizardmen fell over dead. Grey Cloak pulled his weapons free and returned his attention to his brother.

Dyphestive hammered away, headbutt after headbutt. The ogre's jaw sagged, and he swayed. With a fierce expression on his face, Dyphestive hit the ogre one last time. The ogre dropped Dyphestive, stumbled back into the wall, tripped over his own feet, and fell down the steps, taking two lizardmen with him.

"Goodness, your skull really is made of iron, isn't it?" Grey Cloak asked.

Dyphestive picked up his war mace and wiped the blood from his nose. "I think so."

Together, they faced the hoard of lizardmen charging the water-slick steps.

Grey Cloak smiled. "Let's do this." He launched himself into the fray.

30

U p to their necks in lizardmen, Grey Cloak and Dyphestive battled against the hoard. Dyphestive crushed a lizardman's chest with his war mace. His back-swing took out another with a blow to the head. With feline prowess, Grey Cloak weaved through the knot of swarming bodies without suffering a scratch. He ducked, stabbed, slid, and blocked, dropping lizardman after lizardman with fatal strikes of his sword and dagger.

More lizardmen poured in from the back entrance.

Grey Cloak could have sworn that an entire army had been set against them. "We can't keep this up!" he said to Dyphestive.

"I can!" Dyphestive fired back.

Out of nowhere, a hoard of prisoners blindsided the

lizardmen. The angry mob plowed into the shocked lizardmen and drove them to the ground.

It was the break they needed.

"Dyphestive, get the striplings!" Grey Cloak said. "Zora, Streak, it's time to go!"

Streak zigzagged through the lizardmen's feet and climbed up Grey Cloak's back. He was too big to fit in the hood anymore and nestled on Grey Cloak's shoulders.

Grey Cloak winced. "Easy with those claws." He quickly scanned his surroundings as he fought on. The lizardmen slowed as they came in the back door and lined up on the ledge and stairs. Another score of them stood on the main floor, trying to kill Grey Cloak, Dyphestive, and Zora, but over twenty prisoners had joined the fracas. The iron gate was still down and barricaded by the lizardmen on the other side, and even more of their forces had gathered. The only way out was fighting. "So much for a subtle rescue." He looked at Streak, who was facing him. "Any ideas?"

Streak yawned.

"I thought so."

Zora threw the keys up to the prisoners in the cages. One prisoner unlocked his cage and threw the keys to the prisoner in the next cage. It started a chain reaction, and the prisoners dropped down onto the lizardmen and attacked.

Grey Cloak fought back-to-back with Zora. They cut down their foes one by one.

Then the scraggly-haired hermit wandered into the fray. The hermit was very tall, with a rangy build. He picked up a lizardman and hurled him into two others. His golden-brown eyes locked on Grey Cloak. "You are really bad at this."

"And you are really bad at gratitude." Grey Cloak thrust his sword into another lizardman's chest. "Do you have any better ideas?"

"No, I like this one." The hermit ducked away from a lizardman's club, spun around, and elbowed the lizardman in the snout. He snatched up a club and beat on another foe.

As Grey Cloak cut down another lizardman, he said to Zora, "He's very quick for a hermit. Not as quick as me but quick."

Boom!

The bars of the dungeon cells rattled.

Two lizardmen went flying overhead.

Boom!

The head of Dyphestive's war mace, Thunderash, pulsated with energy. With an arc of light, it struck like lightning and popped like thunder.

Boom!

The striplings clung to Dyphestive's back as he knocked a path through the lizardmen and headed toward the stairs. His face was filled with glee as he landed one bone-shattering blow after another. The lizardmen scrambled over one another to get out of his path. "Come on!" he roared. "I'm making a hole!" He rushed the stairs and hit the first lizardman at the bottom with a mighty swing.

Boom!

With all eyes on Dyphestive, Grey Cloak dug his fingers into the wall that led up to the back door and scaled it like an ant. His fingers easily found purchase on the rough grooves and notches, and Zora followed. He slid onto the lip and found himself facing the backs of the gaping lizardmen. He crept behind them and pushed two of them off the ledge.

Zora pushed a third lizardman off the ledge and poked her head around the back door. "The way is clear. Hurry!"

Dyphestive crashed through the last lizardman and made it to the top of the steps. The glowing head of Thunderash faded. The lizardmen on the dungeon floor gathered their courage and made pursuit.

Dyphestive pummeled the lizardmen who reached the top of the steps, one after another. The fighting continued all over the dungeon floor between lizardman and prisoner. The force of lizardmen was stronger, and they started hauling the prisoners back into their cages.

"We have to go!" Zora waved them toward the door.

Grey Cloak patted Streak on the head. "Do your thing."

Streak's throat rattled. His body warmed like a biscuit on Grey Cloak's shoulder, and a stream of thick yellow smoke spewed from his snout.

Grey Cloak stepped in front of Dyphestive and held Streak out with his hands. "Back off, lizardmen. I have a dragon, and I'm not afraid to use him!"

Streak's stream of smoke thickened, filling the dungeon with a yellow fog. The watery-eyed lizardmen choked and coughed. They swung blindly at the air.

Zora and Dyphestive fled through the back door. Grey Cloak backed into the passage, with Streak still spewing smoke thicker than soup. Together, the group wound their way up the narrow, twisting stairs and past passages and doorways. They took a door that exited into an alley behind the huge cathedral and then fled into the night.

Grey Cloak glanced over his shoulder one last time as they ran back to their hideout. None of their pursuers appeared. He patted Streak on the back and smiled.

31

With a smile as broad as a river, Grey Cloak stacked coins in piles of twenty on the wooden table nestled against the wall. The gold and silver chips, as they were often called, shined against the candlelight. Hundreds of coins covered the table and even more filled a small chest, along with three potions in vials.

He was inside a cozy apartment nestled on the outskirts of Monarch City. Crane had set them up in the well-furnished abode, which was very comfortable, with gnome rugs, goosefeather beds and pillows, and plenty of blankets to keep them warm.

Zora, wearing a dark-red silk robe, wandered across the apartment floor and filled two ceramic mugs of coffee before setting the metal urn on the table. She pulled back a chair and sat down beside Grey Cloak.

"The best part is that we don't have to share it with the Wizard Watch," he said as he scooped the coins toward him. "It's all ours."

Zora tapped her painted fingernails on her mug. "Do you think it was worth the risk?"

"Of course I do. Why do you ask?" Grey Cloak asked.

"For one, we could have died, and we probably made enemies with the Dark Addler."

"Pfft... the Dark Addler. I'm not worried about the Dark Addler. If they want the Gunthy striplings so bad, then they can kidnap them again." He rested his face on the piles of coins. "We did our bit. We've been paid, and we're all the better for it. Besides, I wasn't worried. Were you?"

"Your plan didn't work." Zora sipped her coffee.

"My plan did work. The Gunthys are free, and so are we. Sure, we had to improvise a couple of times, but we pulled it off. We always do."

Zora nodded, but she wore a frown.

He pushed a stack of gold coins toward her. "Come now, Zora. This is what we live for. Go and buy yourself something pretty, like a gold tooth or something."

"A gold tooth? Are you saying something's wrong with my teeth?" She placed her hand over her mouth.

"No, of course not. I'm only jesting with you. You're very insecure. Relax and have fun." He flung a stack of coins in the air. "We're rich!"

"You're getting cocky."

He shrugged. "Perhaps that's because I'm getting better at this. Besides, I feel happy." He grabbed her hand. "Why aren't you enjoying this? I figured you of all people would be happy."

She pulled her hands away. "I don't know. I feel like what we did with Talon before was more meaningful."

"How is rescuing striplings not meaningful? Did you see how happy the Gunthys were? Why, their faces were as bright as the sun. I've never seen orcs with smiles so big."

"Lythlenion had a big smile," Dyphestive commented. He lay on a sofa made of crushed velvet that could barely contain his body. His big legs hung over one of the sofa's plush arms, and his head rested on the other.

"Look who woke just in time to join the argument," Grey Cloak said.

"It's not an argument. It's only a discussion," Zora responded.

Dyphestive sat up and hung one arm over the back of the sofa. He wiped the drool from his mouth. "If Grey Cloak is involved, it's an argument."

Grey Cloak held a hand innocently to his chest. "Why am I the bad apple? Because I like saving people for money? Well, if that's the case, perhaps the two of you don't mind parting with your share." He reached for the chest.

Zora slammed the chest lid shut and tucked it under

her arm. "I earned my lot, and so did Dyphestive. We all did. And we need to stop bickering."

"Who's bickering? I'm trying to enjoy our rewards, and you're dragging the moment through the mud. What's wrong with you, Zora?" The moment he said it, he wished he could take it back. He could see anguish on Zora's face, and that anguish quickly turned to anger.

"There is nothing wrong with me!" She stood, turned the chest upside down, and poured it over Grey Cloak's head. "Enjoy your treasure! I'm leaving." She stormed across the room, opened the door, and slammed it behind her.

"She'll be back. Very soon." He started picking coins out of his clothing.

"I don't think she'll be back," Dyphestive said in his deep voice. It had gotten much deeper over the past few months. "She sounded pretty mad."

"She'll be back."

The front door opened. Zora wandered back in with her head down. She still wore her silk robe that showed off her legs. She slipped into her room and closed the door, and after a few moments, she emerged wearing a full set of clothing, her sword, and her dagger belt.

"Zora," Grey Cloak said, without giving her a glance, "I want you to know that I'm sorry, even though I don't think I did anything—"

Slam!

"I think you should have stopped at 'I'm sorry,'" Dyphestive said. He stood up and moved over to the bay window that overlooked the city streets. He scratched his head. "There she is, and there she goes. I think she's stomping mad."

Grey Cloak scooped more coins into the small chest. "I honestly don't understand what got her all riled up. And I don't understand why she wouldn't be happy. This has been going well. We've been doing good things and getting paid." He tilted the chest. "Look! Not to mention, we have four more potions to use."

Dyphestive turned. "I thought there were three."

"Yes, my mistake, three. If you don't mind, lock the door. We don't need any more drunk halflings wandering in like last month. Zooks, I didn't think we'd ever get them out."

Dyphestive locked the door and leaned against it. He rubbed his chin.

"Oh no," Grey Cloak said.

"What?"

"You're thinking, aren't you?"

"Well yeah, I'm always thinking."

"No, you didn't used to think so much. Life was simpler then." Grey Cloak sighed. "Out with it."

"Out with what?"

"Tell me your thoughts."

Dyphestive pushed off the door, crossed the room, and sat down at the table. The chair groaned underneath him. He looked Grey Cloak dead in the eye. "I think Zora is scared."

32

G rey Cloak gave his brother a funny look. "Scared? Scared of what?"

"Scared of us."

Grey Cloak sat down. "I think that is the dumbest notion you've ever come up with. Why would she be scared of us? We're her friends, and we protect her."

Dyphestive picked up Zora's coffee mug and drank it down. "Let me ask you this. When we were fighting the lizardmen, were you even scared?"

Grey Cloak shrugged. "Not really. I didn't even think about it."

"I wasn't scared either."

"But we're well trained. The Sky Riders taught me to be fearless, and I can only imagine the Doom Riders did the same for you."

Streak crawled up on the table and sniffed the piles of gold with his nose. He scooped a mouthful of chips into his mouth, jumped off the table, and scurried away. Grey Cloak chased after the runt dragon, who darted into a hole in the wooden wall. He grabbed the dragon's tail and pulled. Streak's paws dug into the wooden floor and scraped it up.

"Streak, get out of there." Grey Cloak set his feet against the wall and pulled harder with a grunt. "Ugh! Streak, I command you to return those chips."

"Didn't he earn his own share?" Dyphestive asked.

"Whose side are you on? Get over here, and give me hand. He's burrowed into the wall like a gopher."

"I'm not touching him. The last time we went through this, he bit me." Dyphestive rubbed his hand. "Let him have it. You can get it later."

Grey Cloak let go of Streak, and the dragon's tail slipped inside the small hole. He could hear the dragon's claws scratching against the wall. He shook his head. "He's like a mouse squeezing its chubby body into a little hole." He pointed at his brother. "I'm taking his gold out of your share."

"You know that dragons like treasure the same as men."

Grey Cloak dropped down into his seat at the table. "Maybe so, but where is he going to spend it?"

"Why does he have to spend it?" Dyphestive stared at the hole in the wall. "Perhaps he likes it the same as a person would like a painting or a sculpture."

Grey Cloak rubbed his temple. "Your thoughtful considerations are making my skull ache." He rolled his neck. "But please elaborate on our problem with Zora."

"I think she's scared that she isn't like us. After all, we are naturals or the children of naturals. We have a gift that she doesn't, and perhaps, we make her feel, uh... I can't think of the word for it."

"Insecure?"

Dyphestive nodded.

Grey Cloak leaned back in his chair. "I guess that's possible, but Zora is a very capable woman. And this is what Talon does. We adventure. Each of us bring our own strength and skill to the group."

"Maybe she doesn't feel needed."

"Will you quit thinking so much? Let it be, man!" He felt his cheeks warm. Dyphestive's musings were growing more common, and it was getting under his skin. He didn't understand what had happened to his brother, but he missed the simpler man Dyphestive used to be. "Why don't you worry about you? Zora can worry about Zora, and I'll worry about me. How does that sound?"

Dyphestive lifted his mammoth shoulders. "I only wanted to help."

"Do you think you've helped?"

"No."

"Good, I don't either." Grey Cloak shoved some coins across the table. "Fill your pockets with the distinct sound of rare metal kissing rare metal. That will make you feel better."

"The love of gold can lead to destruction."

"Is that so? Is that what you were thinking when you took your gold to the butcher, bought a hog, and had the entire beast roasted to fill your belly?" Grey Cloak raised a brow. "Where was your golden vanity then?"

"That was different. I was hungry."

"You ate the entire pig. No one is that hungry." He stood up and patted his brother on the shoulder. "It's your money, and you can do as you wish with it, but don't feel guilty for earning it. Goodness, the Gunthys would have paid ten times more to have their children back. Couldn't you see that?" He picked up the three potion vials and eyed them. "They got a bargain."

Dyphestive eyed the vials with a squeamish look. "What kind are those?"

"Hmmm..." He ran his fingers over the raised markings on the ceramic. The vials were small and tubular, with colorful wax poured over the corks. "How nice. We have one that will shrink a man, another that restores wounds, and finally... interesting."

"What? I hope it's not that rock skin again. That tasted awful."

"No, this one is for *flying*." He handed it to Dyphestive. "You can have it. I'm not really big on flying."

Dyphestive stuck the potion inside the pocket of his vest. "As long as it doesn't taste awful, I'll try it."

Grey Cloak fetched the Cloak of Legends from its peg on the wall. He slipped the other potions into it. He'd become very attached to the cloak. It held onto everything for him, and the potions he put in the pockets wouldn't break. The cloak had powers, some of which he was only beginning to understand.

Someone knocked hard on the door.

Grey Cloak and Dyphestive exchanged a glance. No one had ever visited them before. Crane and Zora were the only ones who knew where they lived. He pulled a dagger, and Dyphestive grabbed his mace. Grey Cloak held a finger to his lips, hoping whoever it was would go away.

Someone rapped on the door again. Then a piece of parchment slid underneath, and footsteps indicated the person had walked away.

Grey Cloak picked up the note and unfolded it. He read it out loud. "You're dead men. Signed, the Dark Addler."

33

"How many prisoners did we lose?" Finton Slay asked. He was pacing the dungeon where Grey Cloak and Dyphestive rescued the Gunthys.

"Five, including the children," the leader of the lizardmen guards said. He held his pipe in his hand and walked three steps behind Finton Slay. "We rounded up all the other prisoners and put them back in their cells. More of my guards are searching the streets for the escapees."

Finton Slay walked by the cells. He was an older man, slender and bald, who wore black robes, neatly pressed, with a tall, tight collar. He held his hands behind his back, and he moved easily. He didn't come alone either. A dozen men in crimson robes, the same as his, escorted him into the dungeon. All of them wore iron masks with devilish expressions on their faces.

"Five prisoners lost. Tsk tsk tsk, that is unacceptable," Finton Slay said. He ran his fingers over the cell bars. The prisoners he passed cowered in the back of their cells and didn't dare look at him.

"We'll find them. I swear it," the lizardman said.

"No, no, you won't. Your job is to guard them not to hunt them." Finton Slay passed by the ranks of lizardmen standing at attention in the middle of the dungeon. He faced the four-armed ogre that anchored the end of the row. The ogre's nose was busted flat, and his face was swollen like a balloon. "What happened to this one? It looks like he smashed his face into a wall."

"I didn't see everything, my lord." The leader of the lizardmen swallowed. "He battled a human of great girth with light hair. The man was very strong and slayed many of my men with a war mace that hit like thunder. They took us by surprise and used a variety of magic."

Finton Slay lifted his chin. "Magic, you say?"

"Fire, ice, and smoke, and there was a small dragon. A deadly beast."

"I see." Finton Slay walked up the stairs and joined the ranks of his escorts. He turned and faced the lizardmen that waited at the bottom. "Are you certain all these prisoners are secure?"

"Yes, my lord. I swear they won't be going anywhere," the leader of the lizardmen said.

"Good to know." Finton Slay glanced at the cages

suspended in the air. They no longer held prisoners. "It looks like you need to fill those cages."

"As you wish, my lord."

Finton Slay stepped beyond the threshold of the iron gate and said under his breath, "Kill the guards."

Concealed blades slid out of the masked men's sleeves and filled their hands with shining steel.

"Kill them all."

FINTON SLAY STARED at the broad back of his commander, Irsk Monco, who was bent over a basin of water, washing his face. Irsk Monco reached backward. Finton Slay handed him a cloth towel.

Irsk Monco straightened his back, revealing his towering height. He stood almost seven feet tall. He dried his face and handed the towel back to Finton Slay. Irsk was an odd man, one of a kind, people said, part goblin and part elf. His build was lanky but strong, his ears pronounced and pointed, the same as his nose, and he wore the broad smile of a crocodile. He was ugly but carried himself with ease as he moved over to the chair in his study and sat down in the leather seat. He crossed his legs and checked the brass buttons on his shirt. He tapped his long fingernails together. "Five escaped prisoners. Tell me more about them," he said in a scratchy voice.

"The Gunthy children were saved. A nameless hermit slipped out—the guards knew little about him. The other two were a man named Jakoby, a former knight of the Monarchs, and a woman from the Ministry of Hoods named Leena. They were enemies of the state. Imprisoned for life."

Irsk Monco snapped his fingers, making a loud *pop*. He swiped his long, stringy hair to the side of his face and let it hang over one eye.

An ugly little gnome with bright-yellow eyes and a pointed beard wandered into the study with a bowl of black walnuts. He set them on the table, bowed, glared at Finton, and hurried back out.

"Mmmm." Irsk Monco plucked a single nut from the bowl and crushed it in the palm of his hand. His nimble fingers separated the shell from the meat. He stretched his hand toward the bowl. "Would you like one?"

"Of course." Finton Slay helped himself to a black walnut and squeezed it in his hand. The nut was as hard as a rock. He put the walnut in the pocket of his robes. "I'll save it for later."

"The fruit of the nut I do enjoy." Irsk Monco chewed his food on one side of his mouth and dusted the shells off his clothes and onto the floor. "Did you replace the guards?"

"Yes, Master Monco."

"Good. Lizardmen and ogres. They are limited in their

faculties but normally excellent guards. I hope you made an example of them.”

“Of course. Yes, the Iron Devils took care of that. They had the new guards drag the old guards’ bodies away.”

Irsk Monco pointed a finger at Finton Slay. His dark eyes sparkled. “That is exactly what I would have done. So tell me, what do you know about these mercenaries who swiped our prisoners from right underneath our noses?”

“They came with power and clearly overmatched the lizardmen. A human warrior of great strength and an elf armed with magic. Also a woman who could vanish and a runt dragon that smoked the dungeon up.”

“Very interesting.” Irsk Monco sawed his index finger underneath his lips. “There are very few who would cross the Dark Addler. Yet they did. And this isn’t the first time we’ve heard rumors about this group, is it?”

“No, Master Monco. Their descriptions match those of the ones who stole the Sunfire Blossom from the waterway trenches.” He cleared his throat. “What would you have me do?”

Irsk Monco pointed a finger at him. “I would have you do what you think I would do.” He waved Finton away. “That is all.”

34

Two days later, inside Talon's apartment, Crane was freshly returned and fuming. His cheeks were flushed, and he wrung his hands as he paced. "What did I tell you about crossing the Dark Addler? I said, don't do it."

"You said many things," Grey Cloak said, "and I vaguely remember that being one of them." He was sitting on the sofa, his legs crossed, an elbow resting on the arm. "You said not to swim with the walruses either and something about not pinching dwarven ladies."

Dyphestive sat on the other side of the couch, his big body sinking deep into the cushions. He ate a strip of dry beef and washed it down with cider. "You're the one who sets up our missions. I thought you were careful to avoid the Dark Addler."

"I didn't set up this mission." He pointed a pudgy finger at Grey Cloak. "He did."

Dyphestive turned his gaze on his brother. "You told us that Crane set up the contacts."

Grey Cloak shrugged. "Does it really make a difference who sets it up? All that matters is that the Gunthy children were saved."

"The Gunthys have a blood feud with many Monarchs. And just so you know, they are kidnappers too," Crane said.

"Really? They seemed like very nice people," Grey Cloak said.

"They are crooks. And now you've drawn the Dark Addler's attention." Crane held the note up and waved it in front of their faces. "This is not good news."

Grey Cloak raised an eyebrow as he studied the note signed by the Dark Addler. He smirked. "Wait a moment. That's your handwriting."

"What?" Crane looked the note up and down. "Well, it's similar but hardly a match."

"It's yours," Grey Cloak said matter-of-factly.

Crane gave a clever smile. "So it is." He set the parchment down on the table. "See how I changed my letter endings on the 'D' and the 'A'? I wondered if that would throw you."

Dyphestive leaned forward. "So the Dark Addler's not going to kill us?"

"Try to kill us," Grey Cloak said.

"Now don't get ahead of yourselves. Word of your brazen rescue is being whispered in the backrooms and alleys," Crane said in a hushed voice. "You've created a stir, and they will come for you. I wrote this note to get you on your toes. And here you are, sitting like dead ducks, waiting for the enemy to bust down your door."

Grey Cloak pulled a nail file from his cloak pocket and started filing. "We've been keeping an eye out."

"Do you ever take that cloak off?" Crane asked.

"When necessary." Streak crawled onto the couch and nestled in Grey Cloak's lap. "The cloak is very comfortable."

Crane shook his head and resumed pacing. "Listen to me. No more missions while I'm gone. I have to set them up because you don't know this town."

"We've been here over a year," Grey Cloak said.

"Yes, and I've been here most of my life. I know the families, the monarchy, the hierarchy, and the pecking order. And the Gunthys, despite what you think, are not good people, not that the members of the Dark Addler are either. Now they all know your faces, and they'll be coming." He wiped his mouth with his hand. "No more missions unless I approve them."

"We can't sit in this apartment all day long. That's boring," Grey Cloak said.

"Yes, boring," Dyphestive agreed.

"You have plenty of money. Spend it. Isn't that what you

wanted, to be free and enjoy the pleasures that this splendid world has to offer?"

Grey Cloak ran his finger over Streak's black stripes. The dragon's scales were warm to the touch. "Well, that was fun, but it's not..."

Crane stopped and bent an ear toward him. "It's not what?"

Grey Cloak didn't respond, but Dyphestive did. "It's not what he thought it would be."

"Ah," Crane said with bright eyes. "So, a chest full of gold isn't everything?"

"It's clearly not everything, but if you are going to force me to admit it, no, it's not as fulfilling as I hoped it would be."

Crane gave an approving nod. "Is that how you feel, Dyphestive?"

"I don't care for the treasure, but I admit that I do enjoy the comfort it brings. But we can't sit here day in and day out doing nothing. We need to use our—"

"Talents? Abilities? Yes, yes you do. Instead of trying to line your pockets with riches, why don't you lie low, find real work, and be normal until I return?"

"You're leaving?" Grey Cloak asked.

"I have to. That's what I do."

"But we need another mission to stay sharp."

"Then practice what I'm preaching, and use more discretion over the next few months."

"Few months!" Grey Cloak stood up. Streak's claws bit into his thigh. "Gah! Will you stop doing that, Streak?" He peeled the dragon away from his garments and set him on the couch. "You're telling us no more missions for months?"

"I'm leaving you with a mission."

Grey Cloak and Dyphestive exchanged doubtful glances.

"What mission?" Grey Cloak asked.

"Find jobs. Lie low. That's your mission."

35

"Order up! Order up!" a hard-nosed orc shouted from behind the bar of the Tavern Dwellers Inn.

Grey Cloak hustled between the tables of the rustic inn that smelled like applewood and bacon. He wiped his hands on his apron, swung by the bar, and deftly lifted a tray loaded with platters of food onto his shoulder. He squeezed his way through the busy tavern and started serving the women at a table.

"Ladies," he said politely as he unloaded the plates in front of their hungry eyes.

There were four women in all, a human, an elf, an orc, and a halfling, each dressed in garish clothing and decorated with fine jewelry. Each was pretty in her own way, but it wouldn't have hurt them to miss a meal either, as their buttons strained to keep their clothing fastened.

"You had the smoked venison," he said as he set it on the table, "and you, the candied ram, and for the elven maiden, a bowl of farm-picked vegetables and gnome-crafted cheeses."

The orcen woman smacked her lips as she palmed her fork and knife and sawed into her meat.

The halfling woman patted Grey Cloak on the bottom and said in a rusty voice, "Don't forget the dessert later, cute thing." She winked at him.

The other women cackled like hyenas then turned their attention to their food and gossipy conversation.

Grey Cloak refilled tankard after tankard of ale, goblets of wine, and pitchers of a dark mead that only the hardiest customers drank. Sweat glistened on his forehead, and his heels started to burn inside his boots.

He waited on customer after customer and studied every detail about them. His keen eye accounted for diamond earrings and gold jewelry. They wore jewel-studded bracelets and necklaces of pearl. A fortune walked through the doors day and night and spent money, lots and lots of money on food and drinks. The thriving citizens of Monarch City practically gorged themselves.

Drunks' coins spilled from their pockets. Women staggered out of the tavern and sometimes were carried home unconscious. All sorts of revelry and dancing occurred. But to Grey Cloak's surprise, no one stole a thing. Not one single item was reported missing because the wealthy citizens were protected by the watchful eye of the Tavern Dwellers Inn owner, Aham the Watchful.

A rough voice caught his attention. "Grey Cloak."

He turned around and found himself face-to-face with Aham the Watchful. Aham had a shapeless, gelatinous body with many tentacles that had an eyeball on the end of each one. Aham was a slink, a race of people that dwelled underground but could thrive on the surface. Their wobbly bodies were disturbing to look at, and their demeanor was gruff, but they were outstanding observers. "Take some time. You work hard. I'll call you back."

He nodded. "Thanks." Without another word, he escaped into the kitchen.

A full crew was hard at work preparing meals. Most of the races were represented, and the young women he worked with were quite fetching.

He squeezed by a cute woman with lots of curls in her hair. In a flirty voice, she said, "Hi, Grey Cloak."

"Hi, Cammie," he said with a wiggle of his fingers. His eyes lingered on hers, and she vanished into the front room. He made his way to the back, where Dyphestive stood over a huge iron pot and stirred the contents with a wooden spoon as big as a shovel. "Are you enjoying your new work as much as I am?"

Dyphestive's mammoth shoulders rolled. His apron was coated in food and flour, and his hair was a mess. "They tried to let me cook, but Aham said this is all I'm good for."

Grey Cloak leaned over the pot. "All you can do is stir the dough?"

"He said I keep getting in the way. It's not my fault that I'm not squishy like him."

"You aren't squishy at all." He hopped up on a table and sat down. "It could be worse. At least you aren't dealing with a bunch of grabby halflings. That same one keeps pinching my bottom, and then her friends hee-haw like donkeys." He rambled on. "The dwarves and orcs never tip, and they always argue about it. And I didn't realize that elves could be so cheap. I thought they were more... gracious. But no, they're pickier than the dwarves. This is awful. I'd rather be working with Rhonna. How long are we going to do this?"

"It's only been two days."

Grey Cloak hung his head and sighed. "I can't do this another day."

"We're doing it. This is how we lie low and stay out of trouble. Besides, I like it. I'm meeting new people and learning new things."

"There really is something wrong with you. I'd look for another job, but I'm too tired to try. Can't we just not work?"

"You know what Crane says about idle time."

"Yes, I know."

"Grey Cloak!" Aham slid across the floor toward them. "Get back to work."

"So soon?" He slid off the table and dropped to the floor like a stone, his head held low.

Aham pushed him down the kitchen aisle with his many tentacles. "Scoot! Scoot! Scoot!" The eyes on his back tentacles locked on Dyphestive, and his mouth twisted from the front of his globular body to the back. "Who said you could stop stirring? Get at it, dunderhead!"

36

With his arms dragging, Grey Cloak headed toward a table in the back where a new patron had arrived and sat with her back to him. The scene at the Tavern Dwellers Inn had finally started to wind down when the new customer arrived.

Don't these people ever sleep?

Without so much as a glance at the customer, he rattled off his customary introduction, the standard peppiness in his voice gone. "Welcome to the Tavern Dwellers Inn, home of the best stew in the city. We offer many spirits. Would you like to start off with some ale or wine? We have a wide variety."

The woman at the table started giggling uncontrollably.

He gave her a serious look. "Zora!" Even though she was laughing at him, he couldn't be happier to see her.

"Aren't you a sight for my tired eyes?" He sat down. "Where have you been? I've missed you."

"I like your apron. Not a speck on it. Impressive." Her eyes scanned the room. "You've picked a very interesting occupation."

"Seriously, where have you been? It's been days. I was worried."

"I could tell by how many doors you beat down."

"Oh, come now. If I had looked for you, you would've been insulted. You know that I know that you can take care of yourself." He grabbed her hand. "Dyphestive will be thrilled. He's in the back, breaking dishes. I'll get him."

She grabbed his hand and held him fast. "No, we'll catch up later. Listen, I'm sorry that I blew my skull over our conversation. I've been embarrassed. That's why it's taken me so long to come back. I feel like a fool."

He sat back in his chair. "Whoa. I never imagined that you'd admit it."

The muscles in her jaw tightened. Through clenched teeth, she said, "Admit what?"

"I mean, you know, you can be hardheaded, and I didn't expect an apology so soon."

"You arrogant, snobbish, immature, stupid, foolish little elf!" She pulled her hand away. "And to think that I was trying to mend fences."

"What did I say wrong? You said that you felt like a fool,

and I agreed. But I don't think you're a fool, just in that moment."

Zora stood up from the table. "Have a good night, Grey Cloak. And please, tell your brother, the smart one, hello for me." She stormed through the tavern and vanished out the doors.

Grey Cloak shrugged. "What did I say?"

DYPHESTIVE WANDERED outside into the alley with a jug of cider in his hand. He dabbed his sweaty forehead with a dishrag and drank from the jug, gulping down the contents.

Glug-glug-glug—

A loud racket erupted the silence. Someone had fallen into the wooden food-delivery crates.

"Get out of here, vagrants, or I'll bust you up." Dyphestive wore a few hats at the tavern. He washed the dishes, carried anything heavy, mopped the floors, and managed any trouble in the alley. He tracked down the man who had fallen into the crates. He pulled the disheveled man up and pinned him against the wall. "You can't be here. Move along."

"You can't be here," the man fired back. He was exceptionally large for a vagrant. "Let me go."

"I'll let you go if you promise to leave." Dyphestive

squinted. "Say, you're the hermit we ran into in the dungeons." He pushed the man harder against the wall. "What are you doing here? Following us?"

"No. Maybe," the hermit said in a gruff voice. "I'm hungry. Feed me."

"I can't feed you. I'll lose my job."

"Give me a drink. Only one drink."

Dyphestive felt a tug on his heart. He let go of the hermit. "I'll give you some cider, but then you have to go. Understand?"

The hermit scratched his head and rasped, "I'm too tired to think."

Dyphestive handed the hermit his jug and peeked inside the back door. "If Aham sees me doing this, I'm really going to be in trouble."

The hermit chugged the cider down. He gasped loudly. "Ah! That's good!"

"Will you be quiet? Aham has ears in his eyes too."

"Who is Aham?"

"The owner." Dyphestive reached for the jug. The hermit cradled it to his chest. "Give that back. Aham doesn't miss a thing."

"Fair enough." The hermit tossed him the jug. "Now get me something to eat."

Dyphestive rolled his eyes. "You said that you would leave."

"But I don't have anywhere to go." The hermit lowered

his voice and spoke with his scaly hand shielding his mouth. "I am an escaped prisoner. They are looking for me." His eyes darted back and forth. "I am hiding and hungry. Besides, I haven't eaten since you let me out. I'm your responsibility. You must feed me."

"Horseshoes." Dyphestive took another look inside. "I'll buy some bread from Aham and give it to you when I leave. Wait here until I'm finished. Do you understand?"

The hermit pointed at the ground. "I'll wait right here."

"No, hide in the crates so no one else sees you. I'll be back." He stepped inside, closed the door, leaned against it, and sighed. "Why does he keep popping up?"

37

Grey Cloak rolled out of bed and stretched toward the ceiling. He twisted from side to side and rubbed his arms. It was morning, and he could hear the roosters from the farmlands crowing. Unlike his counterparts, Dyphestive and Zora, he wasn't much of a sleeper. He needed rest but never a full night's sleep even when he was exhausted.

He put his bare feet on the floorboards and made his twin bed. On the other side of the small room, Dyphestive was curled up underneath a fur blanket. He looked like a bear lying on a small rug. He'd come in last night a little after Grey Cloak had, which was normal because Dyphestive had to clean the tavern tables and floors.

Without making a sound, he slipped from the room and peeked into the one just down the hall. Zora's bed was empty. It had been for days, but everything was neatly kept. The bed was made, the corners of the blankets tucked tight. The room had a small vanity and an oval mirror. Her hairbrushes and a small jewelry box sat neatly on the vanity's top. A wooden footlocker stood in front of her bed's footboard. A body-length mirror was propped in the corner.

He sighed as he stared into the dimly lit room. "As Aham would say, I'm a dunderhead." It had taken him the better part of the night to figure out what he'd done to upset Zora. Finally, after thinking about some of his conversations with Anya, it became perfectly clear. He'd opened his big mouth when he should have kept it closed.

I didn't really do anything wrong. I only agreed with what she said. Why is she so sensitive? Are all women so touchy? He shrugged. *Probably.*

He wandered over to the small kitchen and prepared a pot of coffee on the stove. He didn't care for eating or drinking, like most people did, but coffee he could enjoy. It smelled so good, and it warmed him from head to toe.

He pulled the curtains back and looked down on the streets below. The early-bird merchants were rolling their carts to their designated spots along the cobblestone streets. Farmers rolled in on wagons loaded with canisters of milk, stalks of sugarcane, and fresh fruit and vegetables, making deliveries to restaurants and taverns. The morning was one of his favorite times to stroll the streets. It gave him a feel for everything going on. He noticed a pretty group of women in long cotton dresses, jogging down the streets and giggling with one another. They were farmers delivering baskets of eggs from the outlying barns.

It made his back tighten to think of the work he would have do again at the Tavern Dwellers Inn. It was almost as bad as working at Rhonna's forge, possibly worse, as the spoiled people could be ridiculously picky and even more demanding.

A prickling sensation made the hairs rise on his arms.

Where's Streak?

Normally, the runt dragon would lie on Grey Cloak's feet until he fed the dragon. The dragon's body was toasty, and it kept his toes warm in the morning. "Where is that rascal?" He turned and froze.

Someone lay huddled underneath a pile of blankets on the sofa. The body filled the length of the couch, but they were too big to be Zora. At first, Grey Cloak thought it had to be Dyphestive, but he had seen his blood brother sleeping soundly in their room moments before.

Who in the world?

He reached into the kitchen and grabbed a broom leaning against the wall. Using the top end, he lifted the blankets away from the man's face. An open golden-brown eye stared right back into his face. It was the hermit from the dungeons. "You!"

"Yes, me. Now go away. I'm trying to sleep." The hermit covered up again.

Grey Cloak flipped the broom around and started beating the hermit with the bristles. "Get out of here! Get! Get! Get! Dyphestive, get out here! We have an intruder!"

Dyphestive stumbled out of the room in his trousers. His tired eyes widened. "What's going on?"

Grey Cloak kept hitting the hermit with the broom. "What does it look like? We have a hermit intruder. Now, quit standing around. Pick him up, and throw him out! I'll open a window!"

"Grey, calm down. I told him he could stay," Dyphestive admitted.

"You what?" Grey Cloak continued to hit the hermit, but his blows were much softer. "Why would you do such an insane thing?"

The hermit sat up and snatched the broom out of his hand. "Because he's kind!"

"Give that back!" Grey Cloak stole the broom back.

The pair of men, young and old, went back and forth, grabbing the broom from one another.

Dyphestive stepped over and tore the broom away from them. "Stop it!" He eyed them. "I let him stay because he needed help, and he's not such a bad person."

"He's a hermit who attacked us," Grey Cloak fired back.

"And helped us. Remember what he did for Zora?" Dyphestive reminded him.

"Yes, but that was a long time ago. I didn't trust him then, and I don't trust him now." Grey Cloak scanned the room nervously. "Streak, where are you?" He eyed the hermit. "Did you eat him?"

The hermit uncovered the blankets. Streak was curled up on the sofa where the hermit's feet had rested.

"Streak, you traitor," Grey Cloak said with anguish.

The hermit set Streak on his lap and petted the little dragon. "He's not a traitor but a fine friend with excellent judgment of character." Streak flicked his pink tongue out. "You are very blessed to have him, and you chose wisely."

Deflated, Grey Cloak pulled over a chair and sat down. He looked the hermit straight in the eye. "What is going on?"

38

"Steal a dragon, save the world," the hermit said.

Grey Cloak rolled his eyes. "You've said that, and we've done that. We stole a dragon at Crow Valley. We stole and freed one at Dagger Ford. What more do you want?"

"Wrong place. Wrong time. Wrong dragons," the hermit said.

"Horseshoes, will you tell us what you want us to do?" Grey Cloak leaned forward and took a closer look at the man. Underneath his rugged exterior, complete with scraggly hair and a beard, the hermit had strong, handsome features. His frame was sturdy and stooped, and his dark scaly skin was ugly, but otherwise, he looked pretty formidable for a hermit. "And what is your name, if you have one?"

The hermit lifted a finger, pointing a long yellow fingernail at the ceiling. "Well, my name is not important. Names rarely are, and my birth name is very, very, very, very long, but to keep it short and simple, you can call me Thanadiliditis."

Dyphestive gave an approving nod. "I like it. Much better than hermit."

"It's too long. How about Than?"

Thanadiliditis nodded.

"Than the Hermit it is." Grey Cloak continued. "Now will you please tell us why you're bothering us?"

"Because I need your help," Than said.

"What sort of help?" Grey Cloak asked.

"I need your help to return home."

Grey Cloak and Dyphestive exchanged puzzled looks.

"You seem very able for a hermit. How hard could it be to return home?" Grey Cloak asked. "Are you from the shelf or some unknown part that is more exotic?"

"The latter," Than said. "I am from another world entirely."

"I see." Grey Cloak hooked Dyphestive by the arm and dragged him toward the small patio that overlooked the city. "If you'll excuse us, Than." He closed the patio door behind him. "He's out of his skull. Get rid of him."

"What? Why?" Dyphestive argued. "We should help him."

"Help a madman? I don't think so. Besides, Crane

warned us about meddling in the lives of others until he returns."

"Ah, so now you want to listen to Crane." Dyphestive crossed his arms and eyed his smaller brother.

"What? I've been listening for several days. I have a job, and I'm staying out of trouble. And now this?" He poked his brother in the chest. "Maybe Crane is testing us. Huh? Did you consider that?"

Dyphestive fingered his chin thoughtfully.

Grey Cloak smacked Dyphestive's hand down. "I hate it when you do that."

"Why?"

"It's misplaced with your brawny build. Just don't do it, and spit out what you're thinking."

"I think we should hear him out."

"You're determined to entertain a hermit. Great. I'll tell you what, we'll hear him out, and if we don't like what he says, we'll toss him out on the street."

Dyphestive gave him a disappointed look. "You should be nicer to people."

"I would be if they bathed more." He opened the door and resumed his spot in his chair. "Than, *we've* decided to entertain you story, so please continue."

"I'll try to make it short, seeing as you're so very busy serving tables." He cleared his throat. "Anyway, I'm not from this world. I, like both of you, was an adventurer of sorts. A portal opened that bridged my world to yours. In my world, it's called a mural. I was sucked into it and separated from my family and friends."

Grey Cloak shrugged. He could buy into the other-world scenario because of what he'd discovered with the Figurine of Heroes. It brought people from other worlds to this one. He wondered briefly if that might have had something to do with it, but he didn't mention it. He caught a look in Dyphestive's eye and gave him a warning glare.

Than continued. "Ever since I arrived, I've been trying to find a way back home. In the process, I've learned a great deal about this world and how it operates. After all, I've been here a very long time. I have a theory about what is happening to my world and how Black Frost is involved."

"You know about Black Frost?" Grey Cloak asked.

Still petting Streak, Than said, "I know a lot about dragons, and being from a world not so different from this one, I can see things that others might miss. I believe that Black Frost is feeding on the magic in my world. The very same portal that I came through, he tapped it. As a result, my world is dying while Black Frost is thriving. But it's only a theory."

"How did you come up with this theory?" Grey Cloak asked.

"When I first came through the portal, I arrived in Dark Mountain. I stayed there for quite some time, trying to find a way home, before I took a new direction and fled."

"I see. And I imagine you can't prove that any of your story is true."

"I promise I'm not lying. I'm only asking for your help, not gold."

"Why us?" Grey Cloak asked.

"Even though you're arrogant and self-centered, you still have enough sense to know the difference between right and wrong." Than looked at Dyphestive. "You're not arrogant or self-centered. You are strong and loyal, but your blood brother, well, he's difficult."

"How did you know we're blood brothers?" Grey Cloak asked.

"It's obvious. Besides, you just admitted it." Than let out a warm chuckle. "You aren't as clever as you thought, are you?"

"Yes... I mean, no... I mean... I refuse to answer that."

Dyphestive chuckled.

"Laugh it up, ham head." Grey Cloak frowned. "Again, why us?"

"Because you did something that none of the other stripling Riskers even thought about let alone attempted. You escaped from Dark Mountain... and I helped."

39

"You helped?" Grey Cloak and Dyphestive sat up and said simultaneously.

"Like the two of you, I have the ability to speak with the dragons." Than patted Streak on the top of his flat head. He traced the outline of the dragon's little horns with his fingers. "You see, there are dragons in my world too."

"Seeing how grand dragons can already talk, that isn't so impressive," Grey Cloak fired back.

"True, but they don't talk to just anyone, do they?" Than's rust-colored eyebrows crinkled. "But they talked to me—well, at least one of them did. Bonfire."

Dyphestive caught his breath. "You knew her?"

"If you'll remember, Bonfire didn't speak to anyone for years. She only slept. My whispers woke her when I became privy to what the two of you were up to." Golden flecks burned in Than's tawny-brown eyes. "She hated Black Frost. It didn't take a lot to convince her to help you."

"But why else?" Grey Cloak asked.

"You are foolish but brave. And you understand the importance of freedom. That concept is not something you were taught. You were born with it because you come from good stock. Both of you." Than brushed the stringy locks of rusty-red hair away from the side of his face. "My hair looks horrible, doesn't it?"

"What?" Grey Cloak asked.

"Never mind, I try not to think about it." Than cleared his throat. "Ahem. Er... could I have some coffee?"

"I'll fetch it," Dyphestive said.

The blond blood brother was hanging on Than's every word, but Grey Cloak wasn't buying it. He had too many questions that needed answers. He chose to keep his mouth shut and listen but only because of Streak's fondness for the man. Otherwise, he would have tossed the hermit out on his rump by then.

"Thank you. As I was saying," Than continued after Dyphestive handed him his coffee, "in order to defeat Black Frost, I believe this world needs heroes who are young at heart and will do anything to protect their freedom. The people of Gapoli must be able to exercise free will before evil stamps it away. I've seen what happens when good men turn a blind eye to the horrors that befall others. While they're lost in their own ambitions, the rug gets pulled out from under their feet, and a pit of despair opens below them."

The truth of Than's words moved Grey Cloak's heart. His glance into his brother's eyes told him Dyphestive felt the same. His throat dry, he said, "The Sky Riders have vowed to kill Black Frost. Do you know how they can do it?"

"No. Not with any certainty. I will tell you what I do know. The portal that Black Frost feeds on is inside his temple, deep in the belly of the earth. It's the most heavily guarded location in the world, right in the heart of Dark Mountain. One would have to find a way to close the portal. That would stop Black Frost from feeding on it. Or killing Black Frost would close the portal."

Dyphestive leaned forward. "You've seen the portal?"

"Aye, I came through it and tried to swim back. My only choice at the time was to flee for my life or try again. I'm perhaps the only person outside of Black Frost's elite that has seen it and lived." Than's chin dropped. "I fear I made a grave mistake when I missed my opportunity to jump back through."

Grey Cloak slapped his knees. "Well, this is simple. We just need to tell the Sky Riders what to do, and they can come up with a plan to handle it."

"Simple, hah. The Sky Riders are noble but short-sighted. Their pride is what blinded them in the first place, and Black Frost turned their own kind against them. You must be wary of who you work with. I've approached the

Wizard Watch to gain insight. They are a secretive lot. Their forces are divided, so be very careful who you trust."

Grey Cloak's thoughts lingered on Tatiana. It had been a long time since he'd seen the beautiful elven sorceress. He'd expected her to show her face like she had before, not long after they arrived in Monarch City, start bossing them around, and take them on a quest for dragon charms, but it hadn't happened. In truth, he was relieved. He'd been enjoying his freedom, and he quickly realized that he didn't want to give it up. Not to save the world and not to save anybody. He would kick it down the road for the Sky Riders to handle. All he needed to do was get word to Anya.

Than stared intensely at the blood brothers.

"What?" Grey Cloak blustered.

"I get the feeling that you aren't taking me seriously."

Grey Cloak combed his hair behind his ear. "We have to be objective. After all, you've told us a story, but you don't have any proof of this."

"If my words ring true, have faith and follow them," Than replied.

"What do you expect us to do? Sneak into Dark Mountain, close the portal, and kill Black Frost?" He giggled. "That would be a suicide mission, even for us. But we'll get word to the Sky Riders. We have people. And didn't you tell the Wizard Watch about this?"

"They didn't believe me either." Than set Streak aside and rose. He really was very tall for a hermit, as tall as

Dyphestive. "Not to mention, some of them tried to kill me, and they'll probably try to kill you, too, if you tell the wrong members of their brood. Wizards. There are so few you can trust." He neatly folded up the blanket and draped it over the back of the sofa. "Everyone has ideas of how to kill Black Frost. An old saying from another world goes, 'There is more than one way to skin a cat.' Keep an open mind, and use your imagination. Remember, anything is possible." He headed for the door.

"Why don't you try to stop him?" Grey Cloak asked.

"Don't think that I'm not trying. I'm digging for information and entrusting what I learn to you. If only I still had my youth. Listen to me, bold youths. Black Frost gets stronger. I know this because I grow weaker with every passing day. My world is dying. I can feel it in my bones." Sadness filled his eyes. "I need your help, and so does the rest of the world." And with that, he left.

Grey Cloak picked up his chair and tucked it into the table. He looked at Dyphestive. "Shew, I didn't think he was ever going to leave."

Dyphestive shook his head and disappeared into his room. He closed the door behind him.

"What did I say this time?"

40

It had been a quiet night at the Tavern Dwellers Inn, as the fall festival had come. The festival was a celebration of the seasons as well as an opportunity for all the races to show off their wares and unique talents.

Grey Cloak had finished with his last customer, a heavyset orcen woman dressed in lavish cotton robes and beaded jewelry. She had bags under her eyes, and her bare arms were flabby. She'd ordered a sample of every dessert from the menu.

Aham stood behind the bar, counting coins with his gelatinous tentacle hands. He put the coins in a sack and stored them inside his body. All the while, he mumbled, "Money, money, money. I love money."

After another hard night of work, Grey Cloak rolled up the long sleeves on his white shirt and hung his apron in the kitchen. Dyphestive was in the back of the kitchen, dumping wasted food into bins. Using a wagon in the back alley, another worker would haul the waste to the hogs. Grey Cloak tried to make eye contact with his brother, but it didn't happen. Ever since Than the Hermit had left, Dyphestive had become frosty.

Grey Cloak went back into the tavern's main room. A few barmaids were still putting chairs up on tables. Grey Cloak grabbed a chair before a cute human girl did. She had bouncy locks of blond hair and long eyelashes. "Teena, why don't you go home? I'd be glad to do this."

With a smile, Teena rose up on tiptoe and kissed him on the cheek. "You're the sweetest. See you tomorrow?"

"Where else would I be—"

Teena was gone before he finished the sentence. The other two barmaids waved at him and thanked him. It left him alone with the last customer, the orcen woman, who waved him over with a large meaty hand.

Oh, great. She wants more to eat. I'd bet anything.

"Can I help you?" he asked.

"Do you have a moment to sit down?" she said in a bubbly voice. She pushed a chair out and patted it.

He looked over his shoulder and didn't see Aham. His feet were burning, and he wouldn't mind a break. He took a seat. Looking at all of her plates, he asked, "Are you sure you don't need anything else?"

"No, everything was delicious." She dabbed her full lips

with a napkin and let out a small belch. "Excuse me."

He covered his nose. "It's fine. I'm used to it."

"My name is Orpah. I'm from out of town and here for the fall festival." She wiggled in her seat, and the chair groaned beneath her. "I'm an artist."

Grey Cloak nodded. "That's great."

"Would you care if I drew you a picture? You inspire me."

Rubbing the back of his neck, he said, "Well, I, uh, should probably get back to work. My boss is not very patient."

"It's only a sketch, and I'm very quick." Orpah grabbed a pad of parchment and a small basket containing ink and a quill from the next chair over. The bracelets on her thick wrists rattled as she moved. Her chubby fingers were nimble and quick as the quill scratched across the parchment.

Surprised at her deft hand, he leaned toward her and tried to take a look.

"No peeking," she said.

"You appear to be very good."

"Does that surprise you?"

"Well, yes."

"Is it because I'm such a beautiful woman?"

Lords of the Air, no! "Er... well, your striking appearance does have something to do with it. You wear so much jewelry." *And your fingers are very meaty.*

"Oh," she said with delight, "you like my jewelry, do you? What else do you like about me?"

Oh my, what do I say to that? She's beastly. "Um, I don't know. You have so many qualities. I don't know where to start."

"You have a clever tongue. I like that about you. What's your name?"

"Oh, Grey Cloak."

"That's an interesting name." Orpah's bracelets jangled loudly on her wrists. Her hand moved very fast, and her eyes were intense. "Tell me, Grey Cloak, what is such a handsome young man like yourself doing working in a place like this?"

"I've been asking that myself." Even though Orpah wasn't the most pleasant woman to look at, she was easy to talk to. Her words drew him in. "Just passing the time, I guess. I'm pretty young, and I haven't really settled down."

"I see. Well, the picture is finished. Would you like to see?"

"You have me on the edge of my seat."

Orpah turned the picture around.

Grey Cloak's eyes widened, and his heart jumped. It was a picture of Zora. His blood ran cold.

The bubbly tone in Orpah's voice turned into something much more sinister. "If you want to see her alive again, fetch your big friend and come with me."

41

The floor was cold, and the air damp. Grey Cloak's knees quavered. He'd been kneeling for over an hour with a burlap hood covering his head. He could hear Dyphestive breathing and the fiery crackle of torches burning. He and his brother had been told to keep silent and were left in the gloom. He knew they were not alone. Guards breathed quietly and fought to stand still. He visualized ten of them.

This is getting old.

He twisted against the knots keeping his hands tied behind his back. He could free himself but chose not to with so many eyes on him.

Orpah the ogre had departed long ago, but the stink of her perfume still lingered. She'd led Grey Cloak and Dyphestive outside into an alley, where they met up with a gang of thugs that tied them up and hooded them.

That was when the journey to discover Zora's whereabouts became interesting. What Grey Cloak hoped would be a brisk walk to a nearby dungeon turned out to be an hours-long jaunt of twists and turns. They went up staircases and down them. They zigzagged through the streets, crawled through narrow passages, and were even dragged down a tunnel one time. He kept his ears peeled and tried to visualize where he was. He didn't have much luck with that.

However, he did have one saving grace. When Orpah sent him to fetch Dyphestive, he put on the Cloak of Legends. She didn't seem to care.

Dyphestive sniffed and groaned.

"Be still!" a firm voice said.

Grey Cloak heard something smack against what he assumed was Dyphestive's head.

A door's metal hinges groaned. Two sets of soft footsteps entered the room. It sounded like one of the arrivals took a seat in a chair and sighed.

"What do we have here?" a man asked. His scratchy voice carried an edge.

"These are the two men that invaded the cathedral dungeon and freed the Gunthy children," another man said in a polished, matter-of-fact manner.

"Ah, yes, the adventuring interlopers. This should prove

interesting, very interesting indeed," the man said from his chair.

Someone in the room was scraping blades together. Fingers tapped on the arm of the chair. Nuts popped loudly in the hollow silence as they were crushed.

Grey Cloak's skin prickled.

"Did you torture them first, Finton?" the man in the chair asked.

"No, Master Monco. Would you like us to proceed for your pleasure?" Finton replied.

"Hmmm... no, I want them to be at full capability when they talk to me. Remove their hoods."

Rough-handed men yanked the hoods off the brothers' heads.

The torchlight was dim, and Grey Cloak's blinking eyes quickly adjusted. He was inside a stone chamber with a single torch on each wall. Two men stood at each wall, wearing iron masks with fiendish expressions and crimson robes. An imposing figure, very tall, strong, and lean, sat in a chair of steel. His face was elven with fiendish goblin features. His ears were large and pointed, and his dimpled chin was pronounced. He had a mouthful of long teeth. He wore a blue cotton shirt with brass buttons. Grey Cloak saw no weapons on his body, but his fingernails, which drummed the end of his chair's arm, were sharp and long. He also wore Zora's scarf around his neck.

"I am Irsk Monco, leader of the Dark Addler, but if you

mention that to anyone outside of this room, I'll have you killed." Irsk politely gestured to the man standing beside him. The man was bald, with haunting eyes and a ghostly complexion. He wore pitch-black robes that hid his feet and a tight collar. "This is my second in command, Finton Slay. He is the leader of the Iron Devils." He flicked his finger toward the masked men along the walls.

"Speak of him, either, and we'll have you killed." Irsk leaned forward. "Now, tell me who you are."

"Apparently, you already know who we are, or you wouldn't have dragged us into your cellar," Grey Cloak answered.

"Don't be a fool, child. I'm giving you an opportunity to provide more clarity for your position. I would think you would be more accommodating, considering the life of your friend *Zora* hangs in the balance." Irsk grabbed a black apple-sized walnut from the bowl on the table beside his chair. He crushed the nut in the palm of his hand. "In case you were unaware, she doesn't hold up very long when she's tortured."

"You better not harm a hair on her head!" Dyphestive yelled. "Or I'll crush you like that nu—"

Bzzzzt!

One of the Iron Devils rammed a steel rod with a bright head against Dyphestive's back. The jolt stood the brawny youth's hair on end. He teetered but kept his balance.

"Impressive, the youth has a formidable constitution. I can use that," Irsk said. "Now, where were we?"

"Making introductions. I am Grey Cloak, and this is Dyphestive. Of course, you must have known that."

"I'm a busy man. I can't be expected to remember every name and face I encounter." Irsk chewed the bits of nut. "But I do." He nodded at the Iron Devils that stood behind the brothers. "Use the jolter on them. Use the jolter on them both."

An Iron Devil jammed a steel rod against Grey Cloak's back. His body caught fire from toenail to fingertip. He collapsed forward, cracking his chin on the floor.

42

After shocking Grey Cloak and Dyphestive several more times, Irsk said, "Now that I have your full attention, we can continue."

The guards pulled the brothers up off the floor. Grey Cloak swayed, but Dyphestive was as steady as a rock.

Grey Cloak shook his head. "You have our attention. Please don't hit us with that stick anymore. Just tell us what you want from us."

"What do I want from you? My, the one with a smart mouth doesn't have an answer to that? It should be very easy to guess. You owe me several things. Either you can return the prisoners you stole from me, or"—Irsk cracked a nut in his hand—"you can fully compensate me for their value."

Grey Cloak smirked. "How much is that?"

"I'll tell you what, because I'm impressed by your boldness and daring—after all, who is foolish enough to take on the dungeons of the Dark Addler?—I'll settle for a paltry sum of ten thousand gold chips."

"Ten thousand!" Grey Cloak exclaimed.

"I'm not finished." Irsk wagged a finger at Grey Cloak. "And the runt dragon that was in your possession. How does that sound?"

"I'm not giving you my dragon, and I don't have ten thousand gold pieces. No one has that sort of money."

Irsk's face lit up with surprise. "What do you mean? Certainly the Gunthys paid you at least that much to rescue their children. I would think they paid you ten thousand apiece. After all, the ransom was only twenty thousand chips. Tell me, boys, how much did you receive?"

Grey Cloak was embarrassed to say. Aside from the three potions, he had only received a thousand in coins, and they weren't all gold either. "Well, not that much."

"Not nearly that much!" Dyphestive offered.

Grey Cloak stared at his brother, caught his eye, and said without speaking, "I'll handle this."

Dyphestive tightened his lips.

Irsk tapped his long finger on his cheek. "My, my, my, we do have a problem. And it looks like I'm going to have to either kill your dear Zora or sell her into slavery. The trolls of Woonan pay top coin for elves as pretty and delicious as that."

"We don't have that many chips. Why don't you let her go and take me instead?" he suggested.

"And me!" Dyphestive interjected.

"Isn't that noble? So very, very noble. You know, the seers say there is no gift so precious as giving one's life for another. I think it's a bushel of manure, but people believe in all sorts of ideologies." Irsk toyed with Zora's scarf and seemed to ponder it. "I've considered your offer, and the answer is no."

"Why?" Grey Cloak asked.

"I consider myself a good judge of character. You see, the two of you have proven to be very formidable for such young men. Even though the ogres and lizardmen are strong and devoted, they are slow-witted and easy to dupe. But you overcame their strength with your own force and, according to our sources, some noteworthy guile. That's why I think you'll be able to come up with the money I am asking for." Irsk raised his brows. "Can you do it?"

"I've never even seen that many chips."

"Me either," Dyphestive said.

"You disappoint me, both of you." Irsk pointed at Grey Cloak. "But mostly you. I'll tell you what. I'll make it easy for you. If you want to see your friend alive again, you will give me ten thousand gold chips and a runt dragon, or you can complete a mission for me."

"What sort of mission?"

Irsk leaned back in his chair, his huge smile stretching

from ear to ear. "Oh, I'm not going to tell you that. You can either agree or disagree." He opened his hands. "What will it be?"

"We'll do it!" Grey Cloak said.

Dyphestive looked at him like he'd lost his mind.

Grey Cloak knew Dyphestive thought they would be sent to kill someone, but he didn't have a choice. He had to buy time. "Who do you want us to kill?"

Irsk laughed. Finton remained straight-faced while the Iron Devils stayed silent.

"What are you, assassins now? Oh, you make me chuckle." He crushed another black walnut in his hand. "As I noted before, I'm a good judge of character, and the two of you are not cold-blooded killers. Fighters, yes, but not murderers. You see, I work with people's strengths."

"Let me guess. You want us to steal the Gunthy children back," Grey Cloak said.

"Honestly, Grey Cloak, you shouldn't try to read my mind." Irsk tapped his temple. "I'm unpredictable. Besides, the Gunthys were small potatoes. It was more of a vendetta than anything else, and I think a clear message was sent. No, no, no, I have something that will truly challenge your bravado and skill. If you cannot come up with ten thousand chips and the dragon, I will have *you* fetch me something of far greater value."

Grey Cloak's mood brightened. Fetching, which was another word for stealing, was right up his alley, but he wasn't going to jump right in. "Before we *fetch* anything, I request that we see proof that Zora's alive."

Irsk opened his hands. "Fair enough. Finton, bring her in."

Finton snapped his fingers. A door opened behind him, and two more Iron Devils dragged Zora into the room. Her wrists and ankles were bound in shackles. Her hair was mussed. She had a purple bruise on her cheek, and she was gagged. Her tired eyes met Grey Cloak's.

His blood boiled. "You better not hurt her!"

"Don't be so predictable. I'll do as I want if you don't do as I tell you to," Irsk warned. "Take her away."

The Iron Devils hauled Zora, kicking and screaming, back through the doorway. Her head twisted to look over her shoulder as her pleading eyes searched for Grey Cloak's.

"I'll save you!" he called out.

"We'll save you. It's a promise," Dyphestive added.

The door closed, and Zora was gone.

Grey Cloak sneered. "I warn you, you better not harm another hair on her head."

"You aren't in a position to threaten anyone, child," Irsk said as he dusted the walnut crumbs onto the floor. "Set your petty emotions aside while we conduct our business. Can you do that without your skull boiling over?"

"Maybe, maybe not."

"I see. Well, here it is. I want you to fetch me a piece of Codd's armor."

"Who is Codd?" Dyphestive asked.

Irsk gave them both an incredulous look. "How long have you lived here that you don't know who Codd is? Never mind, I'll let you figure that out for yourselves. Fetch me the shield from Codd's armor, and I'll release Zora and call it even. Fail to do so, and well"—he shrugged—"you win some, you lose some."

"Where do we look for Codd's armor?"

"Oh, that's the best part. It's inside the very heart of Monarch Castle. You can't miss it." With an impish grin, he waved his hand. The Iron Devils placed the sackcloths over their heads. "I'll give you three days. Goodbye."

43

"Wake up. Wake up." Dyphestive shook Grey Cloak.

"Zooks, what hit me?" Grey Cloak asked as he opened his eyes. He had a splitting headache. After Irsk Monco covered their faces in sackcloth, someone—he guessed Finton—had gassed them with some sort of spell that made Grey Cloak's world turn upside down. He sat up and rubbed his eyes. "I feel awful. What about you?"

"I woke up a few moments ago. I'm fine, but my ears are ringing."

They were in a dark alley, and the ground was wet and sticky. Grey Cloak lifted his hand out of some sort of puddle. "Uck! Look at us, dropped off like rubbage in a stink hole." His back slid up the wall as he stood. His eyes swept over both ends of the alley. "Let's figure out where we are."

Monarch City was well laid out in a vast network of buildings, roads, and alleys. They'd come nowhere close to exploring all of it. Together, they wandered to the alley's entrance, where they could see the stars shining in the sky. The brightest star of all hung right over the great spires of Monarch Castle. Its great gates loomed only fifty yards away.

"I'll be. They dropped us right where we need to be." He tried to wipe the grime off his cloak. "Ick."

Monarch Castle was nothing short of spectacular. Not only was it the largest structure in the city, it was the tallest one, too, complete with a moat and drawbridge. Its high walls and coppery spires could be seen from any spot in the city. It was said that blood-thirsty spiny-back walruses occupied the moat. The Honor Guard marched day and night behind the battlements of the parapet walls. Their bright armor shined in the starlight.

"An entire army guards that castle. And Irsk wants us to steal a shield from inside that place?" Dyphestive asked. "How will we even sneak in?"

"I can handle that."

Dyphestive grabbed Grey Cloak by the collar of his cloak. "You aren't going anywhere without me. I'm going to rescue Zora too."

"No offense, brother, but this job requires a man with a much lesser build. That's my gift, not yours. Look at what we're up against. You can't go in there and start bashing things. You'll get caught."

"Whatever you do, I will be a part of it."

"Fine, you know that I'll let you know. Now, will you let go of me?"

Dyphestive released him and straightened his cloak. "Sorry. I'm angry. We can't let anything happen to Zora. And Irsk, he made my skin crawl. What sort of man is he?"

"I've never seen the likes of him, but he looked like part elf and part goblin. If Zora's safety hadn't been on the line, I think we could have taken them all."

Dyphestive nodded. "I felt the same way. I wanted so badly to burst my bonds and hammer all of them. What are we going to do, Grey?"

Grey Cloak leaned against the wall and set his eyes on the castle. "I need to get inside." His comment drew an aggravated look from his brother. "Only to scout. I won't try to steal anything unless there's a golden opportunity. I need to try and find the location of this Codd's armor. Apparently, it's common knowledge." He rubbed his temples. "Let's take a moment and think."

The morning star dropped from the sky, and dawn quickly came upon them. Vendors began rolling their carts into their spots along the streets, and merchants opened the doors to their shops. Even though Grey Cloak felt the weight of the world on his shoulders, it appeared to be another routine day for the rest of the world.

Dyphestive's tummy growled so loudly that it startled a cat slinking through the alley. That was when Grey Cloak noticed the strangest thing. Citizens started to line up outside the Monarch Castle's drawbridge. A group of Honor Guards stood beside a lavish wooden booth, where a merchant collected chips from the line of citizens.

Grey Cloak stepped out of the alley, his mouth hanging open. He backhanded Dyphestive in the shoulder. "Come on."

"What are we doing?" Dyphestive whispered as they walked toward the mouth of Monarch Castle.

Grey Cloak pointed at the sign posted on the merchant's stand:

Monarch Castle Excursions. Twenty silver chips per person. Ten silver chips per child.

Grey Cloak grinned as he shelled out the coins to the merchant.

The merchant pinched his nose in disgust, and with a quick nod, the Honor Guard briskly escorted Grey Cloak and Dyphestive away.

44

Dyphestive toweled off his damp head and put on a clean vest and trousers. He sat down on his bed, put on his boots, and laced them up. "I can't believe we were turned away for stinking. That's a first."

Grey Cloak responded from somewhere inside the apartment. "I guess this is what we should expect when we're going to be in the presence of royalty. Are you ready yet?"

Dyphestive buttoned his woolen vest, which was getting tighter around his chest. "I am, but I think I've grown. I'm going to have to find someone to stitch me a new vest. I wish Tanlin were around. He'd take care of it."

Grey Cloak stepped into the doorway. His brick-red shirt was perfectly pressed, and his trousers were spotless. The shine of his black boots made him look particularly sharp. Shaking his head, he looked at Dyphestive. "Once a shepherd, always a shepherd, at least in your case."

Dyphestive checked out his clothing. "What am I supposed to do?"

"Don't worry about it. It will do." Grey Cloak walked over and sniffed his brother. "We'll stop by a lavender vendor on our way there. Come on, we need to hurry."

Streak was curled up at the base of the front door. Grey Cloak bent over to pick him up. Streak growled.

"None of this, Streak. You need to stay where you're safe. There is an evil man out there who wants to snatch you, and I can't have that. If someone comes in, hide." He grasped Streak. The dragon's claws clung to the floorboards. He couldn't pry him off. "A little help?"

"Aw, he looks cute." Dyphestive took a knee, grabbed Streak, and pulled him free from the planks. He walked the warm-bodied dragon to the sofa and gently set him down on a blanket. He patted the dragon on the head. "We'll be back soon. We have to save Zora."

"Thank you," Grey Cloak said. "He latches onto things like a tick. He's getting stubborn. I can't imagine where he gets it from." He exited the room.

Dyphestive rolled his eyes and closed the door behind them. "Yes, I can't imagine where he gets it either."

Grey Cloak locked the door and led the way down the stairwell, which exited onto the bustling streets. They made a quick stop at a lavender vendor before moving on.

Even though he knew his way around the city, Dyphestive was content to follow. He'd always followed Grey Cloak, and even though he was branching out and thinking more for himself, he still trusted his brother. As Grey Cloak walked quickly through the streets, Dyphestive hustled after him. "Slow down, if you don't mind."

Grey Cloak turned his chin over his shoulder, and from the side of his mouth, he said, "Keep up. We're being followed."

"By who?" Dyphestive asked as he turned his head.

Grey Cloak stopped.

Dyphestive bumped into him.

"Quit looking around, will you? You know better than that." Grey Cloak took off again.

Dyphestive kept his eyes forward and hurried after his brother. "Who do you think is following us?" he asked under his breath.

"Think about it. Irsk probably put eyes on us to keep track of our progress. Maybe. I don't know for certain, but I spotted them a block from our apartment. Stay with me."

Dyphestive nodded, and they weaved through the crowds and crossed through alleys between streets. In the middle of one alley, Grey Cloak came to a stop. He pushed Dyphestive against the wall. "Try not to get dirty."

Hunching down, Dyphestive glanced from one end of the alley to the other. At first, he only saw passersby, then a woman appeared at one end of the alley. Her face was covered in a cowl. She had a shapely build, and she wore black slippers.

Grey Cloak elbowed him and nodded at the other end of the alley.

A well-knit man in a traveler's cloak wandered into the alley. A hood covered his face, and he hooked his thumb in his leather sword belt. He made a confident approach.

Dyphestive and Grey Cloak stood back-to-back. Neither of them carried a weapon because the Honor Guard patted down everyone who entered Monarch Castle.

"Listen, friend, you've picked the wrong men to trifle with," Grey Cloak said.

The man walking down the alley put his hand on the pommel of his sword and said forcefully, "We would have a word with you."

"We have more important things to do than have conversations with strangers," Grey Cloak replied. "And you had ample opportunity to approach us in the streets. Instead, you chose to pin us in an alley."

"I have good reason to exercise discretion," the man said.

"Yes, most thieves do."

Dyphestive kept his eyes locked on the small woman before him. She was slighter than Zora, and he was a mountain in comparison. He bent his head forward and caught a glimpse of her hooded eyes. She stared back at him like a wary cat.

"We aren't thieves," the swordsman said.

"Assassins, perhaps?" Grey Cloak responded.

"No."

"Whatever your business," Grey Cloak said, "it will have to wait. We have more important things to do than chitchat with mysterious people in back alleys. Now, if you'll excuse us, we need to get going. That is the polite way to say 'get out of the way.'"

"I'm sorry, but I can't let you do that." The man started to draw his sword.

Grey Cloak jumped the man.

Dyphestive reached down toward the woman. "Sorry, I don't want to hurt you, but if you don't move, I'll—*aaaah!*"

The small woman grabbed his arm and hip-tossed him flat on his back. The violent move knocked the wind out of him. He sat up, catching his breath just in time for her hard side kick to his temple. Stars exploded behind his eyes. He snarled, and his chest heaved.

45

"Listen, little woman, you're making me mad, and you don't want to make me mad," Dyphestive warned as he climbed to his feet. He glared down at the woman who had flipped him in the alley and tried to kick his gray matter out. "I've been hit much harder than that."

The small woman took off her cloak and tossed it aside. Her hair was dark red, almost crimson, and tied back in a very long, braided ponytail. She wore black satin robes trimmed in gold, with a black sash-like belt. Her eyes narrowed with deadly intent. She waved him on with her hand.

He sighed. "You're asking for trouble." Determined not to be caught off guard, he feinted to the right side and lunged to the left, hoping to corral her with his big hands.

She hit his outstretched fingers with a short black stick that was attached by a string to another black stick.

"Ouch!" He flicked his hand, incredulous. "Did you just hit me with a stick?"

The petite woman whipped the strange weapon around her body with blazing speed and showy fashion. It whistled through the air. Flipping the weapon against her waist and over her shoulder, she beckoned him on again with her free hand.

He glanced at his fingertips. "So, you want to play, do you? I'll play." He balled his fists and waded toward her.

Her weapon whistled. She clocked the knuckles on his left hand, busted his chin, cracked his nose, and finished with a hard smack of wood on bone as she connected with his right hand. It all happened in a moment.

His eyes couldn't track her blinding speed. Dyphestive never really intended to harm her or get mad, but now, he was being humiliated. He fixed his gaze on her hands. All he needed to do was grab them and shut her down. He reached.

She rolled her neck, and her long ponytail came to life. It swung around, and a small blade at the end of her ponytail cut him across the eyes. She followed up with a groin kick and busted his head at least five times with her sticks.

Dyphestive staggered back and touched his eyes. Blood came away on his fingers. He lost it and charged her like a bull.

The catlike woman jumped high, flipped over his head, and landed on his back like a monkey. She coiled her long braid around his thick neck and started choking him.

WITH HIS FOCUS on the man's sword, Grey Cloak took a fist to his jaw and staggered back. He rolled on the ground and leg swept the man. The man fell flat on his back with a thud. Both jumped from the flat of their backs to their feet at the same time.

The man's hood fell away from his dark-complexioned face. His cloak opened, revealing a set of studded-leather armor. His neatly combed short black hair matched his moustache.

"Listen to me. I didn't come to fight," the man said. "I came to talk."

From the inner pockets of his cloak, Grey Cloak pulled out a short sword.

The man's eyes widened. "How in Gapoli did you do that?"

Grey Cloak smirked. "I have deep pockets." He thrust his sword forward.

In the blink of an eye, the man pulled his longsword and parried.

They sparred back and forth, their blades connecting loudly with the ring of clashing metal.

The swordsman had a strong arm and great skills to match. He didn't press the attack. He defended himself, parrying every strike Grey Cloak executed. "Will you quit this? I don't want to fight!"

Grey Cloak cut at the man's eyes, forcing him to duck. "You drew first, not me!" He pressed the attack with a series of thrusts and slashes. He might not be the best swordsman in the world, but the Sky Riders trained him better than any. He put on the pressure.

The fighter parried and countered with a quick slash that nearly took off Grey Cloak's ear. "You fight well, but you're overmatched. Can we set our weapons aside and talk?"

"You've wasted enough of my time. If you want to stop fighting, back away and leave us alone!"

"I wish I could, but I can't until you hear me out!" The fighter amped up his game. He unleashed hard, precise strikes that beat against Grey Cloak's sword.

Grey Cloak felt the man's strikes in his wrist. The jarring impact moved up to his elbow and shoulder. His arm started to burn. *Zooks, this man can fight! And I've been trained by the best!*

"Young man, I'm starting to lose my patience with you." Panting, the swordsman backed away, lowering his sword. "I beg of you, please hear me out."

"No." Grey Cloak pulled a dagger from another one of his pockets.

The man took a deep breath through his nose. "Then you give me no choice." The man wrapped both hands around the handle of his sword and advanced.

Grey Cloak braced himself for the man's strike. The fighter squeezed his eyes shut. His sword shimmered with fire. He swung. Metal crashed on metal. Grey Cloak's blades flew from his hands, and an unseen force knocked his body against the wall. He blinked and found a sword pressed against his throat.

46

Spitting through his teeth, Dyphestive reached back and tried to grab the woman's hair.

She bit his finger.

"Ow! Horseshoes! What is wrong with you, woman?" he managed to say despite her attempt to choke him to death with her ponytail. Dyphestive's calm demeanor had long since passed. His blood ran hot. He had been a Doom Rider at one time, trained by the most grueling taskmasters of all time. They beat him. They tormented him, but they never broke him. Now, a wee woman was humiliating him. It was time to turn the tables. "Last chance, lady. Let go, or suffer the—"

With her free hand, she whipped his head with her twin sticks. The blows rang hollow on his skull, like a mighty woodpecker on a tree.

Clok! Clok! Clok! Clok! Clok!

"That's it!" He backpedaled toward the alley wall and crashed into it.

Whomp!

The woman held on tight and squeezed harder. He backed into the wall again and again. She held fast, grunting against the impact. Both hands worked her ponytail as she pulled back with all her might.

Dyphestive growled. He stepped backward and thrust harder with his legs. He hit the wall with a jarring smack. Her gripped loosened, and he went after her again.

Wham! Wham! Wham!

The third time was the charm. The wind went out of her, and her strong grip slipped from his corded neck. She lay on the ground, panting for breath and holding her ribs. She grimaced in pain, but her eyes shot daggers.

"Are you well? I didn't mean to hurt you." He reached for her.

The twin sticks flicked out in the blink of an eye. She hit him square in the crotch.

He doubled over and groaned. "Ooh, right in the nanoos again. What is wrong with you?"

She drew back to hit him again, but this time, he snatched the twin sticks right out of her hands. He swung the sticks at her arm, and the top stick flipped around and cracked him in the nose. "Horseshoes!"

The woman tried to crawl away. He tackled her and

held her down. She clawed her way out of his arms and kicked him in the throat, then peppered him with a flurry of precise kicks and punches.

"Enough, Leena!" a familiar scratchy voice said. "The same for you, Jakoby!"

Everyone froze.

GREY CLOAK COULDN'T BELIEVE his eyes when Thanadiliditis wandered into the alley. He thought he was rid of the strange man.

Than swept his long autumn-brown hair away from his face, and his eyes smiled. "It looks like there's no more need for introductions. You all should know each other well enough by now."

"Than, you set this up?" Grey Cloak asked as he finger-pushed Jakoby's sword away from his throat. "Is this how you introduce people, by letting them try to kill each other?"

"Heh heh. A good grapple never hurt anyone. Don't be so soft. Now you've vetted one another's mettle," Than said.

Jakoby sheathed his sword and caught his breath. "You have strange customs in your world, Than."

"That custom is not from my world. It's from a world far harsher than mine or this one," Than replied.

"How many worlds have you been to?" Grey Cloak asked.

Than shrugged. "It's not important. What is important is that we become better acquainted."

"I don't have time to get acquainted, hermit." Grey Cloak headed out of the alley. "We have a friend to rescue."

Jakoby grabbed Grey Cloak's arm. "Listen, I mostly wanted to thank you and meet you."

Grey Cloak pulled away. "Why?"

"Because, you saved me and Leena from the dungeon. Thanks to your intervention, we escaped. We were a day away from becoming gorka food when you set us free. We owe you a debt of gratitude." Jakoby nodded at Than. "He sent us after you though. I didn't think the meeting would go so poorly."

"So you're working with Than?"

"He recruited us to save the world," Jakoby responded.

Grey Cloak crossed his arms and gave Than a disappointed look. "And I thought you were recruiting us to save the world."

"You know that saying 'beggars can't be choosers'? I'll try mustering all the heroes I can to fulfill my quest," Than said. "At least Jakoby and Leena were willing to listen."

Dyphestive offered his hand to Leena. "Hello, I'm Dyphestive."

She crossed her arms and didn't bat an eyelash at him.

"Does she talk?" Dyphestive asked.

"No, she's all action," Jakoby said with a winning smile. "You got an earful from her, didn't you?"

Rubbing the knots on his head, Dyphestive replied, "It will be a memorable conversation."

"To cut to the chase, I want to offer you my sword, and Leena, her unique skills, at least until we've repaid you for saving our lives."

Grey Cloak gave Jakoby a closer look. Aside from being well-built and handsome, he carried himself with a refined poise. He had proved himself to be a remarkable swords-man, and the thick callouses marked him as a dedicated man with decades of practice. "Tell me, that sword maneuver that got me, what was that?"

"I'm a sword saint. I can draw from my inner core and unleash a precise and lethal strike. I didn't try to kill you, or I would have. I only meant to disarm you, which I did." Jakoby nodded at him. "I hope you understand."

Grey Cloak nodded and turned his attention to the stone-faced Leena. She was pretty but stood like a cat ready to pounce. "She doesn't speak at all?"

"It's not that she can't speak, but I've never heard her."

Grey Cloak smirked at her. "Sounds like a blessing in disguise."

Leena glared at Grey Cloak.

"It appears that her hearing is fine."

"She is a monk from the Ministry of Hoods. I believe she's taken a vow of silence. If I understand it correctly, it aids them in channeling their power. It's similar to my sword craft," Jakoby said. "So, you said you have to save your friend, Zora? Well, you can count us in. If it's the half-elven woman you speak of, we owe her a debt of gratitude too. Tell me, what is it you must do?"

"Steal the shield of Codd and give it to the Dark Addler," Grey Cloak said.

Jakoby broke into gut-busting laughter. "Bwah-haha-hah! That's impossible!"

47

Jakoby regained his composure. "Forgive my outburst, but your quest is ludicrous. Please tell me that this is a jest."

Grey Cloak shook his head. "Irsk Mondo has Zora. We have three days to retrieve the shield of Codd, or she'll be killed or sold into slavery." He picked up his sword and dagger and tucked them away in his cloak.

Leena stormed over and opened his cloak. She patted him down, her eyes wide, and scowled.

He slapped her hands away. "It's magic. Now, go away. Dyphestive, tell your girl to keep her hands off me, will you?"

With a puzzled looked, Dyphestive replied, "She's not my girl."

Than squatted down against the wall and combed his

long fingernails through his hair. "It used to be so beautiful." He caught Grey Cloak looking at him. "I'm sorry about Zora. I will try to help."

"It would help if the three of you would get out of my way," he said. "But you could at least tell me about Codd. Who is he?"

"He is the greatest Monarch Knight of all time, who created the first order of knighthood," Jakoby said with reverence. "I used to be a Monarch Knight until I spoke out against the blasphemy of the Monarchs, which includes many of my fellow knights. I was cast out, accused of being in violation of the knighthood's first order. I'm a fugitive now."

"So, is Codd dead?" Dyphestive asked.

"Long dead, for centuries," Jakoby replied. "But his remains are entombed inside Monarch Castle and on display for all to see. Including his armor, the Armor of Pearl." He drifted off like he was in a dream. "It is a magnificent suit, brilliantly crafted by Codd himself. He is the knight of knights, the perfect man that we all strive to be."

Grey Cloak paced, with his hands behind his back. "Am I to understand that this suit of armor is in plain sight?"

"Yes, and I know what you're thinking. You think that you can steal something that hides in plain sight, but let me tell you," Jakoby warned, "many have tried, and all have failed."

"Sounds like a challenge," Grey Cloak replied. "Let's go, Dyphestive."

THE BLOOD BROTHERS paid their fee at the merchant's stand and were escorted over the drawbridge by the Honor Guard. They went alone, leaving Than, Jakoby, and Leena behind, as they were wanted by the Dark Addler and the local constables. But they weren't the only ones herded toward the castle's main entrance. They rubbed shoulders with many excited citizens.

The group of onlookers oohed and aahed, their toes on the drawbridge as they stared down into the moat. The moat was thirty feet wide and filled with murky water that churned from the girth of the spiny-back walruses passing through. The water-treading behemoths were the size of cows. They had sharp ridges on their broad backs, and their tusks were as long as a man's arm. They were king over the wild gators that swam among them.

One of the Honor Guards was the tour's spokesman. He'd introduced himself as Captain Cleotus, and he wore the uniform suit of scale-mail armor, complete with bracers, shin guards, and a golden sash with his chevron revealing his rank embroidered on it. He always kept his right hand on his longsword's hilt at his left hip. He spoke with a warm and authoritative voice. "If I could please direct your attention to my fellow soldiers posted beside the battlements." He pointed to the soldiers up on the castle wall.

Everyone in the group turned their eyes upward. Thirty feet above, several soldiers stood between the massive battlements of the white-walled castle. They held buckets in their hands.

"Those pails are filled the moat monsters' favorite meal," Captain Cleotus continued. "Cow entrails."

The children on the castle excursion made sour faces and oohed.

Grey Cloak carefully watched as the monsters gathered in the moat along the castle wall directly underneath the soldiers.

Captain Cleotus waved his hand. The nearest soldier flung the pail of innards down into the moat. The spiny-back walruses jettisoned through the dark waters after the chum. Their huge bodies slammed into one another with momentous force. They let out loud snarls and growls like grizzly bears fighting in the water.

The crowd gasped and cheered as the moat monsters tore into the chum and chased one another off. The water beasts brawled over every morsel. One gator was crushed in a walrus's great jaws.

"They sound like you when you eat," Grey Cloak said to Dyphestive. His comment drew a few chuckles.

"Take note, fair citizens and friends of Monarch City,"

Captian Cleotus said. "The moat monsters will eat anything, including you. I'd give you an example today if I could, but we've already fed them our prisoners." He locked eyes with some of the youths. "And bad children."

Their eyes as big as saucers, the children stepped behind the legs of their parents.

Captain Cleotus casually waved his hand, and the rest of the chum was pitched into the moat. With every person's eyes attached to the carnage raging only twenty feet below, he said, "Let's move on, everyone, and watch your step. I would hate for anyone to suffer the same fate as the fellow who fell in during the last excursion."

Everyone quickly stepped away from the edge.

Grey Cloak could see a playful smile in the captain's eyes. "I like him."

Dyphestive chuckled. "Me too."

48

Monarch Castle's great portcullis loomed ahead like a mouthful of steel teeth. The entrance was made up of huge wooden doors they kept closed at night that served to enhance the castle's beautiful exterior as well as protect those inside. The doors were wide open now, with four Honor Guards posted against the oak.

The next barrier was the portcullis drop gate made up of thick bars of steel. Behind it was another set of wooden doors, over twenty feet high, that were open against the castle's white stone walls.

"Everyone, stay together," Captain Cleotus reminded them. "If you'll note, the Honor Guard is keeping an eye on everyone, so please, don't touch or try to pick anything up. This is a fully functioning castle, and the servants will be going about their routine business." He raised a finger covered in a chain-mail glove. "And don't ask them any questions either. I would hate to feed anyone to the moat monsters, but they wouldn't mind at all." He walked backward and spread his arms. "This is the courtyard! Take some time to walk the very paths that your devoted leaders, the Monarchs, take."

The castle courtyard dwarfed what Grey Cloak had imagined. The short green grass stretched along the castle's front wall for a hundred yards and ran another fifty yards deep. The paths were made from gorgeous yellow stones that caught the sunlight and faintly shimmered. Along the paths were many sections that appeared to be used for ceremonies and celebrations. There were stands made of stone and wood and colorful flags with various meanings and symbols. Every place was tagged with a metal pole and a sign at the top of it. Oil lanterns that would light the courtyard paths at night marked every corner.

Grey Cloak breathed in deeply as he passed the most beautiful flowers he had ever seen. The fragrances of the abundant floral life were overwhelming. He grew lightheaded, and a calm came over him. He felt the urge to sit and stare at the brilliant bouquets of flowers and cherry bushes being visited by swarms of humming birds.

"Breathtaking, isn't it?" Captain Cleotus asked. He crept up right between Grey Cloak and Dyphestive, his eyes fixed on the garden.

"Yes, sir." Dyphestive pulled his shoulders back and stood straighter.

"Don't breathe too deeply. The fragrance can make you dizzy." Captain Cleotus gave them both a hardy slap on the back. "Say, the two of you are young and strapping. Have you ever thought about becoming a member of the Honor Guard?" He looked up at Dyphestive. "They love towering men like you. And you never know what that might lead to. You could become a Monarch Knight one day. Shoot, you're almost as big as Codd. Heh heh. Are you still growing?"

"I think so," Dyphestive said.

Captain Cleotus turned his attention to Grey Cloak. "As for elves, we have many, and they are quick learners. The pay is good, and you get the best training in all of Gapoli. Are you interested?"

Grey Cloak played along. This might be the opportunity he was looking for. "Yes, we'd be interested. Do we get swords?"

"Hah, not right away."

"Is this where we train?"

"Yes, but let me warn you, the training is rigorous for a quarter of the year, and you have to prove your worth." The captain pointed at several of the guards posted throughout the courtyard. "Every man and woman here is ready to fight on a single command. Each of them has seen combat in one form or another. Some of them were even adventurers themselves at one time, but they retired for a more routine life."

"Like you?" Grey Cloak said.

Captain Cleotus managed a guilty smile. "I've felt dragon's breath and lived to tell about it. Remember, the Honor Guard are the salt of the city. The ones inside the wall are the elite, and the ones outside can hold their own."

"There are so many of them," Grey Cloak said. "And all of them are good soldiers?"

"The best. Come on. I need to rally the rest of the gawkers. If you think the courtyard is something, wait until you see the inside of the castle. Hah, it has more rooms than I have hairs left on my head." Captain Cleotus elbowed Dyphestive. "Lucky for you, I won't show you them all." The long-legged warrior moved away and rallied the rest of the group.

Grey Cloak held Dyphestive back. "Brother, I have an idea."

"Yes, I know what you are thinking."

"Good." He smirked. "Keep those thoughts to yourself. I'll take it from here."

49

Monarch Castle contained every extravagance imaginable. The sandstone-colored marble walls were dressed with silver sconces containing a mystic gemstone that flickered like candlelight inside. The chandeliers cut from solid crystals that hung from the vaulted ceilings looked like rain and waterfalls.

The grand staircases swept upward and downward in gentle curves that made walking from one floor to another easy. Carpets woven from the finest fibers made the floor as soft as grass underneath the excursion group's feet.

Majestic murals were painted in the domes joining the great intersecting hallways. Captain Cleotus described in detail each and every scene that was painted there: the elves in the fields, the dragons in the grass, the giants from long past. He went on and on, room after room, using his captivating voice to keep the group's attention and make the hours-long trek lively.

Grey Cloak marveled. He'd imagined his fair share of riches in the world but nothing on this scale. Everything, from the smallest vases to the largest sculptures of Monarchs long past, was priceless.

Finally, after over an hour of nonstop walking, the group was allowed to rest their feet in an extravagant living room complete with a sofa and leather chairs so soft and comfortable that several people fell asleep in them. Servants dressed in black, wearing white aprons and carrying silver trays, made their way around the group, serving them sweet cakes with frosting, coffee, and tea.

Dyphestive grabbed a handful of cube-shaped chocolate cakes with pink frosting and popped them into his mouth. "This is wonderful. Better than the Tavern Dwellers Inn, even."

Grey Cloak's eyes were fixed on the fireplace. He was meticulously walking himself through the entirety of the castle. He had memorized every room and corridor. He made particular note of the rooms that were blocked off or sealed with locked doors. One thing that he noticed was the movement of the servants. They came from nowhere, it seemed, as they appeared from behind curtains and out of alcoves underneath the stairwells.

Heh heh heh, passages and secret doors aplenty behind these grandiose walls.

He caught an attractive elven maid, about his age, staring at him. She quickly looked away. When she glanced at him again, he waved. Her hair was in a tight bun, and loose strands hung neatly down in front of her ears. She bent over and refilled his teacup.

"Thank you..." he said, drawing it out to get her name.

She smiled politely and subtly shook her head.

"Oh, that's right. We aren't supposed to speak. Well, my name is Grey Cloak, and it's nice to meet you anyway." He sipped his tea. "It's divine. Hopefully I'll see you around. You know, I'm a server, too, at the Tavern Dwellers Inn."

She smiled, turned, and disappeared behind the curtains.

Dyphestive nudged him so hard, he almost spilled his tea.

"What did you do that for?" Grey Cloak asked.

"What are you doing, flirting with her?" Dyphestive asked.

"I'm not flirting."

"Really? Because you told her where you worked. Why did you do that?"

He shrugged. "I was only making conversation. I don't know. It just came out."

"I'll say. We're trying to save a friend not make new ones."

A pang of guilt fluttered in Grey Cloak's gut. Here he was, trying to hatch a plan to save Zora, and he was making eyes at an elven woman he'd never seen before. She was pretty, however, very pretty. "It's all part of my plan. Work with me."

"Sure."

Captain Cleotus moved to the center of the living room. "If I can have your attention please."

Everyone turned in their seats and fixed their attention on their guide. Many suddenly gasped.

A white eyeball the size of a cantaloupe hovered over Captain Cleotus's shoulder. It had wings like a raven, a pitch-black pupil, and a silver ring for an iris. It had hairy legs like a spider folded underneath it. Captain Cleotus reached behind his shoulder and patted the eyeball on top of its head. "This is a yonder. An all-seeing eye controlled by the Monarchs' personal enchanters. This little fella appears harmless, but he is very observant. Case in point, the yonder has informed the enchanters that one of the members of this group has sticky fingers."

The group exchanged glances with one another.

Captain Cleotus moved toward a heavyset man sitting on a round leather ottoman. He grabbed the man by the collar of his oversized coat and lifted him so his toes dangled above the floor.

"What are you doing?" the heavy man with sagging chins asked. "I didn't steal anything."

A pair of Honor Guards patted the man down. One of them pulled out a silver candlestick from one of the many dining rooms they had toured. Grey Cloak remembered it.

"Sir, you have stolen from the Monarchs. What do you have to say for yourself?"

With the collar of his shirt pinching his neck, the thief managed a clever smile. "It's only stolen if I remove it from the premises, which I haven't."

"I see." Captain Cleotus took the candlestick from the Honor Guard and clocked the man on top of the head.

"Ouch!" the man said.

"Honor Guard, introduce him to the moat monsters."

The Honor Guard hauled the man, kicking and screaming, out of the room.

"Be wary, friends, for the Monarchs have eyes everywhere." Captain Cleotus whistled. Over a dozen yonders popped up from various nooks and crannies in the living room. They were hidden under chairs and tables. Some of them were in plain sight, huddled in the planters or working as bookends. They could change colors and blend in.

An icy chill trickled down Grey Cloak's spine as a yonder rose from its spot on the fireplace mantel. It had looked like a brass ball. Now, it was a fleshy eye that floated across the room.

Cleotus had a warm smile on his face as the yonders

hovered all around him. "Now for the final stop: Codd's crypt. Follow me, everyone."

With twelve giant eyeballs floating above, the creeped-out group with nervous eyes wandered down the hall after the captain.

50

Dyphestive stood with his jaw hanging open, marveling at Codd's crypt. He wasn't the only one. The group was inside a circular room at the back of the castle, where the Honor Guard was stationed. The knight's tomb was a great place, a veritable ring of honor, with marble statues of perfectly sculpted knights from all of the ages surrounding—as if guarding—the tomb.

Even Grey Cloak gawked with bated breath. The coffin itself was unlike anything he'd ever seen. The rectangular structure sat on a massive dais with steps leading up to it. The sarcophagus, made of pure obsidian, was big enough to fit ten men inside. As Captain Cleotus spun a wondrous tale of Codd's heroics, Grey Cloak stared on with fascination.

How big was this man?

Earlier, it seemed that Captain Cleotus had been joking when he quipped about Dyphestive being as big as Codd someday. Codd was a giant among men. Literally.

Grey Cloak swallowed as he elbowed Dyphestive, breaking his brother's stare. "He's humongous." For some reason, he glanced up at the yonders floating above. He quickly counted a dozen creeping backward through the air, attaching themselves individually to the marble pillars and quickly blending with the rock. "I hate those things."

"Look at him. Just look at him. He's gorgeous." Dyphestive couldn't take his eyes off the statue standing on top of Codd's crypt. "He must be nine feet tall."

"Eight, at least," Grey Cloak said. The faceless statue was impressive, but not nearly as impressive as the full suit of plate armor he wore. The metal shined like the morning light hitting the water. The shoulder plates were white and smooth like pearls. The bracers and shin guards matched. Every piece of battle-ravaged armor fit perfectly together, and the boots were shod with iron. The helmet on the statue's head was open-faced, with octagonal angles on the top that perfectly fit the figure's strong but featureless face. Eight spikes decorated the top. A great sword with a pearl handle was sheathed in the armor's girdle, and a huge oval shield with a starburst pattern of metal and pearl sat firmly in the statue's grip. It was at least six feet long.

How am I going to sneak that out of here?

With his fingernails digging into his palms, Grey Cloak scanned the chamber. Twelve statues of knights stood in between the pillars, and an Honor Guard was stationed beside each one. The all-seeing eyes of the yonders and the fact that there was only one way in or out of the tomb increased the weight on Grey Cloak's shoulders tenfold.

He glanced at the statue with Codd's armor again. A feeling of foreboding came over him as he eyed the brilliantly crafted shield. It was fixed tightly in the statue's grip. His ego deflated.

Sorry, Zora, but this is impossible. I'll have to find another way.

"I suppose you all are wondering why Codd is so big, aren't you?" Captain Cleotus asked pleasantly.

Dyphestive spoke up. "I am."

Captain Cleotus continued. "Well, you've probably heard many rumors. You've heard that he was a giant, or part-giant, but that is not true. Many think that magic was used to enhance his great size, but that wouldn't be correct either. No one wants to know the real story about Codd, and that is why we don't show his features like we do the other knights in this room." He waved his arm slowly to indicate the other statues in a showy fashion. Humans, elves, lizardmen, and orcs—both men and women—stood immortalized in stone. "You won't see any dwarves, halflings, or gnomes, as they don't meet the height requirements for knighthood. As for Codd himself, well, he shattered the height requirement that he set. He was a full-blooded ogre, the greatest of them all."

Many of the women gasped. Even Grey Cloak found himself in disbelief that an ogre, a race known for violence and evil, could have possibly founded the Monarch Knights, which were supposed to be the foundation of Monarch City.

"Codd's tale is very long, and the truth is that we don't know all the details. Many of our histories and relics were destroyed centuries ago during the Dragon Siege of 1608. But you can learn more about all of that if you purchase one of our many scrolls in the Monarch Castle's gift shop. Follow me out, and please, come again."

Grey Cloak took one last look as he dragged Dyphestive out by the arm. "Don't get any ideas," he said under his breath.

"About what?"

"Being a Monarch Knight or Honor Guard. We have a serious problem. I'm ashamed to say I don't have any idea how I can pull this off."

"You'll think of something. I have faith in you. What's a gift shop?"

The group was quickly herded by the Honor Guard into the gift shop. It was a store filled with bins and aisles of imitation items and clothing seen inside the castle. The people couldn't shell out their coins fast enough as their children begged and pleaded with them to buy worthless baubles and toys. The striplings fought with wooden swords and shields that rattled against each other. An orcen boy hit his mother in the shin, and she screamed and hauled him out of the store by the ear.

Grey Cloak rifled through the scroll bin with a hollow feeling in his gut. He thought he could handle anything, but now he wasn't so sure, and Zora's life was on the line. He plucked out the Scroll of Codd, a thin piece of parchment with a red ribbon tied around it. Dyphestive tugged on his shirt. "What?" he asked absentmindedly.

"I want to buy this." Dyphestive held up a figurine of Codd that matched the statue and armor down to the last detail.

"Are you jesting? How much is it?"

"Five chips."

"Are you sure you don't want one of those enchanters' wands over there?" he quipped. "It would be more fitting."

"I want this."

"Fine." He fished out five silver coins.

"Five gold chips," Dyphestive said.

"What? Are you out of your skull? Why don't you—"

"I want this. It's my gold, and I'll spend it how I want. Besides"—Dyphestive held it up and examined it—"look at the details. It's remarkable."

Grey Cloak stuffed the coins into his brother's meaty

palm. "That's out of your share, and you better make sure you don't break it. I won't buy you another."

"Thanks, brother."

They paid for the scroll and figurine and departed the gift shop. They were met by Captain Cleotus on their way through the courtyard.

"So, it appears we have a Monarch Knight in the making." The captain eyed Dyphestive's figurine in Grey Cloak's hand. "Have you given any more thought to the Honor Guard?"

"It's not for me, personally," Grey Cloak said. He was still tinkering with the idea that he would have to infiltrate the castle from within. The castle's security had blown his idea to pieces, but he wasn't going to give up yet. "I would be honored to be a servant though." He patted Dyphestive's shoulder. "But I think you've hooked my brother on the opportunity to become an Honor Guard."

"Brother?" Captain Cleotus asked.

"Blood brothers," he replied.

"Ah, men bonded by blood." Captain Cleotus stroked his moustache. "I like it. Meet me at the drawbridge, sunrise tomorrow."

Grey Cloak saluted. "Dawn it is."

"Thank you, Captain." Dyphestive gave a salute of his own.

They were escorted away with the group beyond the castle wall, across the drawbridge, and into the streets.

"Grey, do you have a plan? Do you realize what you signed us up for?"

"No," Grey Cloak replied with a determined look on his face. "I don't know what we're doing, but we're in, and we're going to find a way to save Zora. That's all that matters."

WILL Grey Cloak and Dyphestive be able to save Zora in time?
Can they achieve the impossible and steal Codd's shield?
How is Anya surviving now that she is the last Sky Rider?

AND DON'T FORGET **to leave on review on Book #5, Thunder in Gunder! Review Link Here!**

DON'T MISS all of the pulse-pounding action in *Monarch City: Dragon Wars - Book 6*

On Sale Now! Link!

More details below!

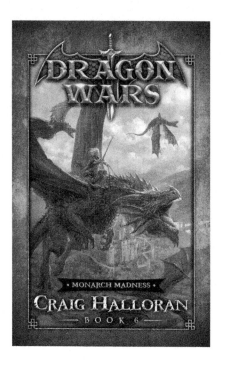

AND IF YOU haven't already, signup for my newsletter and grab 3 FREE books including the Dragon Wars Prequel.

WWW.DRAGONWARSBOOKS.COM

TEACHERS AND STUDENTS, if you would like to order paperback copies for you library or classroom, email craig@thedarkslayer.com to receive a special discount.

GEAR UP in this Dragon Wars body armor enchanted with a +2 Coolness factor/+4 at Gaming Conventions. Sizes range from halfling (Small) to Ogre (XXL). LINK . www.society6.com

ABOUT THE AUTHOR

Craig Halloran resides with his family outside his home-town of Charleston, West Virginia. When he isn't enter-taining mankind, he is seeking adventure, working out, or watching sports. To learn more about him, go to www.dragonwarsbooks.com.

*Check me out on BookBub and follow: HalloranOn-BookBub

    *I would love it if you would subscribe to my mailing list: www.craighalloran.com

    *On Facebook, you can find me at The Darkslayer Report or Craig Halloran

    *Twitter, Twitter, Twitter. I am there too: www.twitter.com/CraigHalloran

    *And of course, you can always email me at craig@thedarkslayer.com

    See my book lists below!

ALSO BY CRAIG HALLORAN

Check out all my great stories...

Free Books

The Darkslayer: Brutal Beginnings

Nath Dragon—Quest for the Thunderstone

The Chronicles of Dragon Series 1 (10-book series)

The Hero, the Sword and the Dragons (Book 1)

Dragon Bones and Tombstones (Book 2)

Terror at the Temple (Book 3)

Clutch of the Cleric (Book 4)

Hunt for the Hero (Book 5)

Siege at the Settlements (Book 6)

Strife in the Sky (Book 7)

Fight and the Fury (Book 8)

War in the Winds (Book 9)

Finale (Book 10)

Boxset 1-5

Boxset 6-10

Collector's Edition 1-10

Tail of the Dragon, The Chronicles of Dragon, Series 2 (10-book series)

Tail of the Dragon #1

Claws of the Dragon #2

Battle of the Dragon #3

Eyes of the Dragon #4

Flight of the Dragon #5

Trial of the Dragon #6

Judgement of the Dragon #7

Wrath of the Dragon #8

Power of the Dragon #9

Hour of the Dragon #10

Boxset 1-5

Boxset 6-10

Collector's Edition 1-10

The Odyssey of Nath Dragon Series (New Series) (Prequel to Chronicles of Dragon)

Exiled

Enslaved

Deadly

Hunted

Strife

The Darkslayer Series 1 (6-book series)

Wrath of the Royals (Book 1)

Blades in the Night (Book 2)

Underling Revenge (Book 3)

Danger and the Druid (Book 4)

Outrage in the Outlands (Book 5)

Chaos at the Castle (Book 6)

Boxset 1-3

Boxset 4-6

Omnibus 1-6

The Darkslayer: Bish and Bone, Series 2 (10-book series)

Bish and Bone (Book 1)

Black Blood (Book 2)

Red Death (Book 3)

Lethal Liaisons (Book 4)

Torment and Terror (Book 5)

Brigands and Badlands (Book 6)

War in the Wasteland (Book 7)

Slaughter in the Streets (Book 8)

Hunt of the Beast (Book 9)

The Battle for Bone (Book 10)

Boxset 1-5

Boxset 6-10

Bish and Bone Omnibus (Books 1-10)

CLASH OF HEROES: Nath Dragon meets The Darkslayer mini series

Book 1

Book 2

Book 3

The Henchmen Chronicles

The King's Henchmen

The King's Assassin

The King's Prisoner

The King's Conjurer

The King's Enemies

The King's Spies

The Gamma Earth Cycle

Escape from the Dominion

Flight from the Dominion

Prison of the Dominion

The Supernatural Bounty Hunter Files (10-book series)

Smoke Rising: Book 1

I Smell Smoke: Book 2

The Red Citadel and the Sorcerer's Power